the burly Q girls

THE 6

Linda Hughes

CHAPTER 1

*L*as Vegas, Nevada, 1995

DOLLY O'DARE hardly dare look at the travesty on stage. But like inexplicably being drawn to the slasher scene in a horror film, she looked.

The stripper slithered her lithe body down the pole like a snake, head down and long legs twitching up in the air like a rattler's luring tail. She wore a scaly G-string, her breasts were bare, and her entire body was slathered in shiny blue goop, no doubt meant to add to her reptilian impersonation. Flailing her tongue in and out, she homed in on the seasoned females sitting in the back of the room and hissed.

Dolly and her two friends flinched and scowled in perfect unison. An Olympics synchronized swimming judge would have given them a 10.

Spilling out onto the floor, the performer – of sorts – morphed into a panther, stalking on all fours to assault the lecherous prey seated around the perimeter of the stage. Ten- and twenty-dollar bills rained down on her in slovenly appreciation, quenching her thirst for profit. She scooped up the moolah, slipped on her stilettos as she stood up, clumsily caught her balance, and counted her take while trouncing off stage.

"That was supposed to be sexy?" Dolly's incredulity radiated from her entire seventy-year-old frame, her normally dulcet voice mocking, her ordinarily erect posture slouched, her usually bright eyes in slits. "What in hell is wrong with those men that they would pay for that?" She shifted her voluptuous body on the small, cheap chair, as if preparing for her own performance. "That's not sexy. What we did was sexy." She straightened her back, lifted her chin, remolded her facial expression, thrust out her arms, and gently jiggled her bosom to emphasize her point. She looked as much like a former prima ballerina as the famous exotic dancer she'd been.

"Ain't that the truth." Ginger Snapper grinned at the memory, nodding vigorously, which caused her curly fire-engine-red-dyed hair to boing about her head.

"I think those poor guys have just never had really good sex. That's the problem. They need a good lay from a nice partner." Sister Merry's feathery voice belied her sympathetic nature.

"Merry, Merry, Merry," Ginger teased in a tone women could only get away with when they'd been friends for a long time, so long they had to stay friends because they knew too much. "You wanna fix the problem and make everybody feel better, like usual."

"That's true," Merry admitted.

"Maybe you shoulda stayed a nun so you could help the needy," Ginger suggested.

"Well, yeah, that's true, too." Merry readily agreed.

Dolly slurped up the remains of her margarita, smacked her

lips, and let loose with a big "Ahhhh, that was good," then got back to the peer review. "We do have to admit that dancer has impressive upper body strength to work the pole like that, but I bet she can't do the splits while leaping over a guitar player while he's playing amazing blues and doing the splits himself." That had been one of Dolly's favorite routines, honed to perfection with blues great T-Bone Walker when they played the same venues. "His jump-blues routine was electric!"

"That was the best." Merry had always marveled at that one.

"Oh, oh. Here's another one," Ginger warned as her gaze veered back to the stage, her eyes widening behind her green-framed glasses. "Holy shit. Get a gander at those bazooms. It looks like the doc stuck beachballs in there. What woman in her right mind would do that to herself? You'd think guys would be afraid to touch them for fear they'd pop."

"I bet she wouldn't ever drown, though." Merry cocked her head to study the object of discussion. "Those babies would pop right up to the surface."

"It's such a shame," Dolly said, shaking her head, "that those girls don't have enough self-confidence to know they can tell any man who doesn't like their God-given boobies to go jump off a cliff."

Three pairs of practiced eyes glommed onto the stripper, watching the woman's body gyrate to ear-splitting hip-hop music while her breasts stayed glued in place. When the performer turned around, bent a-a-all the way down – at least as far as her beachballed chest would allow – and snapped off her G-string, baring her gee-gee, Dolly squished one eye shut and peeked with the other.

"Oh, no. No, no, no," Merry gasped.

"Shee-it," Ginger wheezed.

"That's just plain vulgar. These dancers today don't get it. It isn't 'look at what I've got that you *can* have.' It's 'look at what I've got that you *can't* have.'" Dolly's disgust reached a fevered pitch. "Teasing is what brings them back night after night. Hello-o-o. That's why it's called strip*tease*."

Now the dancer, still half bent over, waggled her pallid bare butt in an illusionary version of a come-hither invitation.

Merry cocked her head again. "You know, her buns look like two loaves of homemade bread, side by side. I'm hungry. Let's go eat."

"Yeah," Ginger agreed, "we're not getting anywhere. Balls ain't here."

Dolly looked around the joint and couldn't help but agree. Dim, dingy, and loud, the place was packed with drooling chumps. Of course, that was to be expected in a place called the Fuzzy Wuzzy. There were a few couples, but they were the only table of all women. Their reason for being there, their third club that night – they'd already tolerated The Pink Padoobie and Tits for Tat – had not materialized. Ballard "Balls" Benedict, Balls Been-a-dick to them, was nowhere in sight. Their agent – former agent now – had absconded with their retirement funds and vanished. These three clients, who were friends after years of performing on the same burlesque circuit, had met up the evening before trying to find him after weeks of unreturned phone calls. The bastard had vanished and taken their hard-earned cash with him.

Seeing that they were living off ether, with only social security checks for Dolly and none yet for Ginger or Merry, getting to Vegas had been a colossal feat for two of them. Dolly had spent three days driving from her home in Detroit. Her old banger of a Ford Fiesta had barely made it. Merry came in from Colorado on a rickety bus. Ginger lived in Vegas, so they were staying at her tiny apartment.

As former burlesque queens they'd made a lot of money in their heydays but had spent a lot, too. They admitted that financial planning wasn't their strong suit, which was one reason they left their retirement planning to their longtime agent and manager. And friend, they once naively thought.

Earlier that day they'd gone to Balls' office only to find it vacated. Not so much as a thumbtack left to stab him with. There was an accountant's office next door but it was closed, so they couldn't even ask any questions. Then they went to Balls' posh condo to discover a fiftyish man who played bongo drums. They didn't bother to ask how one made a living playing bongos and could afford such a pad. In a toke-fueled haze worthy of the hippest of mid-century beatniks, he told them he'd bought the place from some "suga'-wooga" he didn't know and couldn't remember her name.

Not knowing what else to do, the three women resorted to carousing around Sin City, scouring the kind of sleazy strip clubs Balls enjoyed.

In retrospect, they were kicking themselves for trusting the guy with their retirement funds in the first place, except that when they were young and starting out in the business eons earlier, he'd been young and eager, too. He'd been a great agent at first, launching their careers on the burlesque circuit. They had to give him that. Dolly had quickly reached international fame and performed until age fifty. She'd been a club hostess after that. Ginger held her own as a dancer until age forty. She'd been a waitress ever since, with a side practice of doing tattoos, and couldn't wait for retirement a year hence. Merry had a short but successful dancing career during her twenties and early thirties. Since then, she'd enjoyed a satisfying, although not very lucrative, career as a yoga and meditation instructor as well as doing reiki healing.

As time progressed and the dancers retired from the stage to settle into more parochial lives, Ballard Benedict became more and more flamboyant as the years went by. His spiky hair, Porsche, and dazzling white Chiclet smile should have been clues that he'd contorted himself into a guy they barely knew. He'd started to remind Dolly of the sleazy character Rudy Russo in *Used Cars*, the old movie with Kurt Russell. "Trust me" was the salesman's catch phrase while he robbed people blind.

They vowed that the skank would soon discover that betraying three former burlesque queens was a fatal mistake. His sorry ass – well, pecker, actually – would pay. Ginger had brought her tattoo equipment to carry out the deed.

"Okay." Dolly agreed with Merry's suggestion that they eat. "Let's go to that diner down the street. I'm starved."

At the '50s Diner, they were pleased that a booth opened up, seeing that the place was packed, and they grabbed it. As they slid onto the pink plastic seats, they marveled at the tabletop with the black-and-white Formica Boomerang pattern that had been so popular 40 years earlier. The floor was black-and-white checkered linoleum. "Venus" played on the jukebox, which seemed appropriate seeing that the walls displayed '50s movie posters. *The Picnic* with Kim Novak. *A Summer Place* with Sandra Dee. *The Seven Year Itch* with Marilyn Monroe. *Cat on a Hot Tin Roof* with Elizabeth Taylor.

"That was when women were the ultimate sex goddesses, because they had class." Dolly pointed at the memorabilia. The stunning movie stars, with real bosoms in appealing but not too revealing clothing, beamed from the walls, as if encouraging the scammed victims to carry out their plot.

"Yeah, like us," Ginger added. "We had class and were sexy without being gross. And, damn, if we ain't still sexy. Nobody can ever take that away from us. Even if we have gained a few pounds." She pointed at herself and Dolly. Then she pointed at Merry. "You probably weigh what you did back then."

"Well, yeah. But remember, I do yoga and work out and hike and meditate and all that stuff."

"I admire your energy. But you know what?" Dolly shrugged.

"This extra twenty pounds I have these days doesn't bother me at all. I still feel sexy because I'm still me. We are not and never have been prudes. We're not ashamed of our bodies. Yeah, we showed our tits, but our nipples were always covered with pasties. At least we had a little class."

"I loved my pasties." Merry grinned at the thought of the little round pyramids of sequined fabric they used for the sake of a burlesque dancer's version of modesty. And to obey the law in states that required them. "Especially the ones with tassels."

"Ginger, you were so good at twirling your tassels." Dolly chuckled at the memory. "You were great at getting the momentum just right to sling your breasts in opposite directions, so the tassels twirled in opposite directions, too."

Ginger chuckled. "Yeah, it was easy to get them going in the same direction but in opposites, that took a lot of practice. I spent way too much time in front of the mirror getting it right."

"Hey, have you tried to do it recently?" Merry looked from one friend to the other.

Dolly jokingly swatted in Merry's direction. "Hell no. I'm 70 years old. My breasts aren't where they used to be. I doubt they'd cooperate."

Once they finished chortling, Ginger added, "I liked making pasties, too. Remember how we used to sell them to customers and men would stick them on their shirts and foreheads." She slapped her forehead and crossed her eyes.

"And other places." Dolly shook with laughter and the others joined in.

Ginger added, "There was that skin glue we could use to keep them on but chewed up bubblegum worked best."

"Yeah. Those were the good old days." Merry sighed.

A waitress appeared and in a sugary Southern drawl declared, "Amen! I'm all fer the good ol' days." About their age, her dyed-too-dark beehive hairdo, bright red lipstick, and cheery flamingo earrings supported her claim. "I hafta say, y'all look like good ol' American gals, if ya don't mind my sayin' so. Red." She used her pencil to point at Ginger with her tawny skin and bright red hair. "White." She pointed at Merry, with fair skin and long white hair pulled back into a French braid. "And silver." She pumped the pencil toward Dolly, whose brown skin remained flawless despite advancing age – she liked to declare that "black don't crack" – and whose thick hair had turned a stunning silver over the years.

They smiled up at the waitress and Merry said, "I sure do like your hairdo. It's perfect for wearing a tiara. You should get yourself one."

"Well, thank ya, darlin'. Maybe I'll do jes that. I'm Betty, by the way. Now, what kin I git ya?"

Dolly and Ginger ordered hamburgers, which Betty assured them were good and juicy despite being cheap. Merry, the health nut of the trio, asked for a vegetable plate.

After the waitress left, they fell back into their gabfest. "One thing's for sure," Dolly said. "We never exposed our hoo-has to the audience like that girl did tonight. We wore bikini bottoms, more than girls wear to the beach these days. Once we disrobed, we still had clothes on, so to speak. Why, being totally naked is a private thing, meant to be revealed only behind closed doors. Hell, that's what makes getting behind those closed doors with your lover so much fun." She threw up her hands and shook them. "Surprise!"

Betty brought their drinks – 7 Up for Dolly, ginger ale for Ginger, and water for Merry – and paused for a moment to eavesdrop, putting a finger up to another customer to wait a minute. She nodded agreement to Dolly's comment then took her sweet time sidling over to the other table.

"I'm afraid young women don't think that way anymore," Dolly opined as she took a sip of her drink. "Nowadays young women think anything is game. We were naughty but never nasty. But be that as it may, I think we need to let it go," she relented. "Women today do their own thing, just like we did. We might not like it, but they have a right to do it. What we saw tonight wasn't about what we did; it was all about making money. It's a totally different thing even though some people may think it's the same. We were performers and entertainers first, and exotic dancers as a means of doing that."

"Hey, remember Annie Fannie?" Merry asked.

"Oh good god, how could we forget?" Ginger hissed.

"I know we hate her," Merry soothed, "but remember how she looked totally buff but actually had on skin-colored pasties and that patch she wore over her nether parts. It gave the illusion she was naked, especially behind those big feathery fans." She made a swishing gesture to emulate how Annie had fluttered her fans. "You have to admit, that was a great costume. I loved those fans."

"Too bad she was such a flaming bitch," Ginger huffed.

"Yeah, true. But those fans were fun."

"The dancing we saw tonight wasn't any fun," Ginger moaned.

Dolly slapped the table. "That's it. They aren't fun. That's what I object to the most. There's no humor. No lightness. No good times. It's depressing. We were full of life. Joyful! We loved what we did because we genuinely wanted to entertain people – men *and* women. We were professional performers. We weren't selling sex, we were advocating for love and friendship and acceptance and adventure and campiness... and fun. We wanted to share our love of life with the world."

Betty brought their meals and Merry stared at hers. "A veggie plate here is French fries, mashed potatoes with gravy, and macaroni and cheese, with a butter biscuit." She sighed.

Her friends watched to see what their organic gardener vegan pal would do.

Merry shrugged. "It looks good." She dug in.

As they chowed down, Dolly leaned in and gazed at her

companions. Ginger and Merry grasped the shift in mood and leaned in, too.

"This isn't going to work. We're not going to find Balls here in Vegas. He's gone. He's on some island with some young floozy, living high on the hog on a yacht he bought with his clients' money. Our money."

The trio spent the next hour plotting their revenge on one Balls Been-a-dick if and when they found him. Betty brought free apple pie and coffee. When the diner emptied out at one point, she pulled up a chair and served as sideline supporter.

Eventually, Betty went back to work. The plotters left to hit the sack, seeing that it was way past their bedtime. As they trailed out the door, "In the Still of the Night" played on the jukebox. Yeah, Dolly thought, we still have no answers.

Back at Ginger's apartment, Dolly couldn't sleep. After an hour of tussling around on the pebbly couch, she sat up. The biggest problem was that she missed her Otis. Gone two years now, she still had a hard time sleeping without him. Fifteen years of wedded bliss did that to a gal. She often thought he was still with her, not being able to imagine that he was gone forever. Gone gone, she thought of it.

"Well, baby, what do you think? Should we carry out our plan?"

Silence answered.

She looked around. The combination living-room-kitchenette was probably cheerful during the days of *Laugh-In* on TV. But not since. Ginger had every shelf and wall covered in craft thingies she made, plastic flower arrangements, plastic wreaths, and plastic doodads. If Las Vegas ever ran out of plastic – doubtful, but if they did – they could reclaim enough in this little apartment to serve all of Sin City. Dolly grinned at the tacky décor. If it made Ginger happy, that was all that mattered.

A red glow blinking in through the front window illuminated the room. It came from the sign above a watering hole across the street. She considered the meaning of the light, as it seemed to be directed right at her. Maybe Otis was answering her, after all. She looked out at the sign for Sal's Saloon. Maybe Otis and her guardian angels approved the wicked get-even plan. Satisfied, she finally snuggled in and fell into deep slumber as she dreamt about the ecstasy of revenge on one Balls Been-a-dick.

CHAPTER 2

"Okay, here's the skinny on my plan. We need to hire a private dick to find Balls, and I know how we can get the cash to do it. I didn't tell you last night because I wanted to think it over some more. But before I fell asleep it felt like I got a sign from the angels in heaven themselves telling me we need to do this."

Dolly had her companions' rapt attention. The three of them sat at a corner table eating breakfast in the cafeteria at Circus Circus Casino and Hotel. Ginger worked there as a waitress but had taken a week of vacation when her friends came to town.

Dolly pushed rubbery scrambled eggs around on her plate then put down her fork. "I've met with a book publisher I know in Detroit. He's an old friend who has been a soft porn movie producer and erotic book publisher for thirty-five years."

"Were you in porn movies?" Merry's voice cracked at the thought.

"No, no, no. He used to come into a club where I danced and later at another club where I was a hostess before I retired. You know how I went from dancing to being a hostess?" The others nodded. "Well, he and I got to know each other quite well at that club. Sometimes he'd ask my advice about his books or movies. I ran into him last week. Okay, that's a lie. I 'ran into' him because I went to his office."

Ginger and Merry exchanged confused glances.

"What's his name?" Ginger asked.

"Charlie Champ. Not his real name, I'm sure, but that's his professional name and the only one I know. I went to ask him a question."

Ginger took the bait. "Oh my god, wait a minute, what have you got us into?"

Merry's doleful eyes widened in comprehension. "We're going to be in a porn flick?"

"No. Good lord, do you really think I'm that crazy? We're going to write a book. As soon as we get it done, he'll give us an advance of $1,000 a piece. After that, we each get 3% of the net profits."

"A thousand dollars? Wow. I only have $7,000 with Balls in my retirement fund." Merry's career hadn't netted much of an overflow for saving.

"He has $32,000 of mine and I need it. I wanna blow this circus. Literally." Ginger motioned to indicate the cafeteria, which had filled up with families that included thousands of squirming, squealing kids. It felt like they sat amid a circus arena with its wild animals and unruly performers parading around in front of them.

"I've never told you this before," Dolly said, "but Balls has $203,000 of mine."

"Whoa. That's a lot of dough," Merry said, impressed.

Eyes wide, Ginger nodded agreement.

"Yeah, well, I worked long and hard for it. Balls sent monthly dividend checks for five years after I retired, then they evaporated four months ago. When it first kicked in, I needed the money to pay for Otis' medical care. I would've paid anything to make my baby-boo more comfortable in his final years. Since he died, I've needed the money to pay off more old bills. Now the bills are paid, but I want my money so I can travel and buy a new car and maybe even splurge on a new recliner I've been wanting for years." Her eyes misted at the soulful confession.

Merry took Dolly's hand and squeezed. "What will the book be about?"

"Charlie says if we can find six of us to tell the story of our performing years, he's sure it'll be a good seller. We'll need to include the good, the bad, and the ugly. And the humorous. The famous people we met. The entertainers we performed with. The music. The clubs. And...."

"Oh, oh. You hesitated." Ginger was no fool. "What else?"

"Well, our more interesting sexual escapades."

"Holy moly," Merry whistled. "One of those tell-all sex books."

"Yes, but you know us. We won't be sleazy about it. We'll make it fun. We won't use any real names unless the person is dead. We won't tell on anybody who's still alive. We'll use fake names for that. And we'll make sure to point out that we had relationships with men when we were single, the same thing most single girls do. Not one of us screwed around when we were married." She gestured around the table.

Merry snorted. "Yeah, but I've never been married. Not really."

"I know, I know. But that means you've never screwed around while married. Right?"

Merry considered that and nodded.

"And I was only married that one time for four excruciatingly long years," Ginger lamented. "I never cheated on him. I wish I could say the same was true the other way around."

"I know, I know. He was a douchebag. Now," Dolly barreled ahead, "we have to write this book immediately. In fact, Charlie said if we can get the girls together, he'll send down his ghost-writer right away. We'll talk, he'll take notes, and we'll be recorded. Then this ghostwriter will write it up. Like that. Charlie said he can have it on store shelves in a month. He owns his own print shop and a bunch of sex shops where he sells his books. He says he can't publish sexy books fast enough. They fly off the shelves."

"So ..." Ginger scrunched up her nose as she put the pieces together "... some angels in heaven told you to write a sex book to sell in sex shops."

"Yeah, that's it. The gods and goddesses of the universe. And Otis. They sent me a message through the red light that blinked all night through the window, coming from the bar across the street."

"Oh. Kay. Hmmm." Ginger decided to go with the bizarrely heretical premise.

Merry had no problem with it and moved on to a subject that troubled her more than messages from heaven transmitted via a neon bar sign. "Do you really think we can find three more dancers from the old days? Especially decent ones?"

"That sure does leave out Annie Fannie," Ginger noted. "Not that we'd ever invite her, anyway."

The unspoken message was that Ginger had hated Annie Fannie's guts ever since the feathery fan diva had stolen Ginger's boyfriend. It might have been a long, long time ago, but Ginger's memory had not waned. Neither had her loathing.

"I don't know where we'll find more burly-que girls like us, but they must be out there somewhere." Dolly wavered, not sounding convinced.

Silence loomed as they pondered their conundrum.

Back at Ginger's apartment, sitting at her kitchen table, notebook at hand, Dolly jotted down the kinds of questions she surmised the ghostwriter would ask. "The writer will undoubtedly want to know how we got into exotic dancing." She wrote that as #1 on a list. "We can describe the clubs and the music. And the entertainers and famous people we met." She put those down as #2 and #3.

"And the customers hafta be in there somewhere." Ginger was

adamant. "We met so many crazy and funny and interesting people. Nice people."

"But a few mean ones, too," Merry said.

"Yeah, those, too. But there weren't many of those. I loved the customers." Ginger stuck to her guns about including their audience members.

"Sure. Great idea." Dolly allotted Customers #4.

"What about people who hated us?" It was Merry, sad at the recollection. "Every now and then we'd go into a town where there were protesters who claimed we were godless whores. We stuck together and supported each other through those hard times."

That made #5.

"I'll include some of the racist situations I ran into," Dolly added. "Although, there were surprisingly few of those. Now, we have to include our sexual escapades to keep Charlie happy and to get the money. Without that, he won't bite. I plan on telling how to keep a husband happy for years and years." She grinned as she put down Sex as #6. "Otis said he felt like he'd fallen into a heaven of human flesh. But before we go any further, we have to find three more girls. All of this is for naught if we don't."

Suddenly, an impatient knock from outside assaulted the apartment door like a mobster's Tommy gun. Rat-a-tat-tat. Rat-a-tat-tat.

"Who in hell ...?" Ginger got up and opened the door.

Annie Fannie stood there in all her hoity-toity glory.

Ginger glared up at the tall, svelte woman, her shock evident. "What the fuck are *you* doing here?"

Dressed in a designer outfit that no doubt cost more than Ginger's entire wardrobe, hell, probably her entire apartment, the uninvited guest pressed the back of her hand to Ginger's shoulder to nudge her aside. "Let me in. The heat out here is insufferable." She came to an abrupt halt just inside the door, leaving Ginger stuck in the open threshold to deal with the heat. "Well, well, well.

Look … at … this," Annie snarled as she sauntered into the room and stood like a queen looking down her nose at her peons. "The whole gang is here. Hello, girls. It's been a long time."

Dolly huffed. "Not long enough."

"Aren't you going to invite me to sit down?"

"No, Annie, we're not," Ginger stated flatly.

"I haven't gone by Annie since I quit performing. It's Anastasia now." She patted her dyed blond hair, making certain they noticed she had a chichi coif.

"I'm guessing you've never quit performing, one way or another." Dolly stood up to face the interloper *mano a mano*.

Merry hopped up to join the line of defense.

"My, my. What hostility. What did I ever do to make you all so rudely hostile toward me?"

"Gee, *Annie*, I'm surprised you ask, because we know you don't give a rat's ass what we think." Dolly balled up her fists and ground them into her hips, at the ready.

"As for the hostility," Ginger seethed, thirty years of hot anger boiling up unexpectedly, "how about the fact that you lied to my boyfriend about me and stole him away? Huh? How about that?"

"Pfft. Please. He wasn't worth having. I only dated him a few times. You could have had him back. Oh wait. I remember now. He went on to Pussy Willow after me. I guess he liked her … willow." She smirked, amused at her supposed wit.

"You treated us like shit," Dolly growled. "You insulted our costumes and our acts and even our bodies. Like you thought you were so much better than us."

"Well …" Annie made the mistake of throwing her arms out wide and looking around the room. "I've certainly never lived in a hovel like this."

That did it. Ginger flung herself at their tormenter, clawing at the viper's haute couture dress and tearing it down to her waist.

"You little bitch!" Annie Fannie, once the most elegant of exotic dancers, turned out to be a formidable foe. She grabbed a handful of Ginger's hair and with that they hit the floor, rolling around and throwing punches as best they could. Arms and legs flailed about at random, like a game of Whack-a-mole gone bad.

Dolly and Merry jumped into action, each snatching a brawler and yanking her away. Everybody got roughed up in the process. The Women's Wrestling Association had nothing on them.

"Girls! Girls!" Dolly hollered. "This isn't going to change anything."

"Stop! Stop!" Merry yelled at the same time. "You're both acting like Neanderthals."

Once separated and on opposite sides of the room, the brutal enemies tried to kill each other with laser stares.

"Look at what you did to my dress. It's ruined." Annie slung the comment across the room. Her pink, embroidered, lacy, padded, underwire bra poked out at them.

"Yeah. Well, that's nothing compared to what you did to my life. I loved Harold!" Ginger's lower lip quivered as she shook a quaking finger at her nemesis.

Annie frowned, paused, then said, "His name was Howard."

"No, it wasn't! He was my Harold."

"Ah, Ginger, honey." Dolly's gentle tone caused Ginger to look at her friend. "I remember him."

They watched as awareness clicked in on Ginger's face.

"As much as I hate to admit that Annie is right, his name was Howard," Dolly reminded her.

Ginger looked to Merry for support, but all Merry could offer was a helpless shrug.

"Oh. Oh. Well. Yeah, sure. Now I remember." Ginger straightened herself, patted her mussed up hair, casually sat down at the table, and calmly clasped her hands. "I knew that."

"Now that we've done a brawling bump and grind down memory lane," Annie chided, stuffing the torn edge of her dress up into her bra straps, "I'd like to get to the reason for my visit and then get out of this dump as quickly as possible."

"Do tell," Dolly said. "Why in hell are you here?"

"And how did you know where I live?" Ginger wanted to know.

"May I?" Annie pointed to a chair at the table. "This will only take a minute and I promise not to leave cooties or anything."

When no one responded, she sat down. Dolly and Merry followed, so all four of them were on a level battling ground.

"First of all, I got your name and address from the H.R. office at Circus Circus." She swept a hand at Ginger. "Last I knew you worked there and, sure enough, you're still there after all these years."

The snide innuendo that Ginger hadn't gone anywhere in life got a rise out of her. She started to get up from her chair, but Dolly patted her arm. Curiosity won out, as Ginger sat back down to hear what might come next.

"They aren't supposed to give out that type of information, of course," Annie said, ignoring Ginger's latest act of aggressive, "but I easily convinced them I was your cousin and our dear old grandpa had left you some money I needed to get to you. They're idiots."

Ginger merely rolled her eyes.

"As for why I'm here, I need to find Balls. Do you know where he's at?"

"Why do you care about Balls?" Dolly was flummoxed. "I mean, didn't you marry that older, filthy rich guy? Last I saw in the tabloids, he was still as rich as Midas and as old as Methuselah but still alive, and you were still married. What? Did he die and leave you out of his will or something?"

She'd tossed out the catty remark without thought, but the way it landed told them all they needed to know.

"He did. He died and you didn't get anything. Ha."

Annie sat there as stiff and silent as a Vogue magazine cover.

"Hot damn," Ginger mocked. "If you want your retirement fund, you're shit outta luck, just like us lowly li'l ne'er-do-wells."

"What do you mean?" For the first time, Annie looked vulnerable. Human, almost.

"She means he's hightailed it out of here with our cash." Dolly almost felt glad to share the horrible news with this stuck-up bully. "We can't find him."

"But … but I want my money." Annie came alive with surprise.

"So do we, but we ain't getting it until we find him." Ginger stated the obvious.

"What have you done so far to try to find him?" Annie's accusatory tone didn't settle well with her tablemates.

"What have *you* done?" Dolly threw back at her.

"Well, nothing yet. I just got to town. His office is empty. I didn't know where else to go, other than to see if you …" she pointed at Ginger "… knew where he was." Fanning herself with her hand, she switched gears. "I need a glass of water. I'm parched. It's hot in here."

No one moved. She got the hint.

"Okay then. You're telling me you don't know where Balls is at. We're all looking for him. Why don't we join forces?"

"We've got 'forces'," Dolly said, pointing to her two friends.

"Oh, come on. You all can't be holding a grudge after all these years."

"Yeah, we can," Ginger said, sounding a bit like a bratty six-year-old.

"Don't ever piss off a burly-que girl," Merry added.

Annie looked down at her torn dress as the churning in her brain was practically visible. She bit her lip in quandary. She sighed a sigh of forced resignation. She came to a decision.

"Okay. How about this?" she proposed. "I have a penthouse at the Bellagio. The suite has five bedrooms and five and a half bathrooms. A gorgeous living room and kitchen. Balconies all over the place. A hot tub. Room service. Maid service. An open account at the hotel's shops and salons and spa. And in the casino. Come stay there with me while we figure this out."

Dolly squinted at her. "I thought you were broke."

"Personally, I am. At the moment anyway, until I can pay my lawyer to proceed with the lawsuit his fucking son has filed against me, freezing all my assets. If I don't get some cash to the lawyer soon, I lose. I won't go into all the details now, but it means a great deal of money to me."

A thousand questions collided around in Dolly's head, but she decided to save them for later. She wanted to focus on whether they should go stay at the Bellagio. Even if they never found Balls that would be a great vacation, like none she'd ever be able to afford on her own. But they'd have to stay with Annie. Did she and Ginger and Merry want to do that? Her dilemma solved itself when Ginger shocked her.

"Let's go." Ginger popped up out of her chair. "Bellagio, here we come." She grabbed her purse off the kitchen counter.

"Ginger? You really want to do that?" Dolly was confused.

"Why not? I still hate her guts ..." Ginger jabbed a thumb at Annie "... for stealing Harold."

"Howard," a chorus of three reminded her.

"Whatever. Harold. Howard. Frank. I never liked him all that much anyway. I just didn't want *her* to have him. But now I need a break from this apartment and from being broke and from my life. Let's go."

Ginger bounded out the door, leaving it wide open to suck in Nevada's summer heat like a blast from hell. It took a split second for the shock of Ginger's departure to hit home, but the others grabbed their purses and followed. Dolly was the only one with enough presence of mind to grab Ginger's blood pressure meds off the kitchen counter, pick up Ginger's two dancing days scrapbooks, and close the door behind her.

CHAPTER 3

Her waterproof kohl mascara ran down Annie's cheeks like liquid coal. They never expected to see her like this. She'd been bawling uncontrollably for fifteen minutes, sporadically using a towel to wipe her eyes and nose. The towel was doomed, never to see the white of day again.

The four women sat in the hot tub on the balcony of Annie's penthouse suite at the Bellagio, sipping on pricey Dom Perignon Vintage Rosé. A gentle cloud of steam hovered over the water, giving everyone a misty glow. They'd already eaten their filet mignon steak dinners, with braised salmon for Merry, brought up by room service, but were saving the crème brûlée for later.

They'd left Ginger's apartment and ridden over to the hotel in Annie's 1955 Bentley, a well-maintained classic model painted a shiny maroon color. On the way, Annie had informed them that the classy vehicle might be repoed at any moment. She promised the hotel valet she'd give him a big tip to park it "out of sight." Dolly feared that meant the kid would take it drag racing, but she thought it best not to mention that.

Once inside the penthouse, after the three guests had stopped ogling the opulent Italianate décor, Dolly had to ask. "If you're broke, how is it we can stay here?"

"Oh, that's simple." As she talked, Annie touched a button on the wall to turn on music that came from some source Dolly couldn't determine. Frank Sinatra singing *You Make Me Feel So Young* softly filled the room. "All of my money and credit cards are frozen because of the fucking lawsuit, like I said, but that greedy brat doesn't know about the account my pookie let me have here so I could shop. I used to come over every couple of months to have some private time, you know?" Dolly didn't know and if fact couldn't imagine such a thing but remained silent. "But that ogre will figure this out eventually," she whined, gesturing to take in the place, "and they'll shut it down. So in the meantime I want to charge as much as possible to this account. Charge!" She thrust her arm up like a general charging into battle, only needing a sword to complete the picture.

The gesture made her torn dress, which had been tucked into her bra strap, fall to her waist again. Her pink bra glared at them again, unashamedly displaying its armored hold on Annie's boobs.

Ginger ignored the display and put up a hand to indicate "wait." "You mean you invited us here so we could spend as much money as possible to screw your stepson?"

Annie shrugged. "Uh-huh."

The three friends had exchanged a round-robin of looks to calculate what the others thought about this. The unspoken message was clear: take advantage of their arrogant arch-rival for as long as possible. It was their only way of getting even with her for the misery she'd caused them so many years ago.

"Okay, I'm in," Dolly said.

"Me, too," Merry chirped.

"Let's go," Ginger added.

"Hey, can we charge a P.I. to find Balls?" Dolly perked up at the thought.

Annie shook her head. "Afraid not. That was the first thing I asked when I checked in. But we can buy whatever we want in the shops on the property. This is where I do all my shopping. Why there's Bulgari, Dior, Gucci, Valentino. We can get you some luggage at Louis Vuitton. And we'll all get jewelry at Tiffany. You can buy whatever makeup and other stuff you need at the spa. Oh, and there's Prada, Fendi, Chanel ...." She ticked off the names on her fingers as her excitement escalated to the point of manic hysteria. Her companions knew she wasn't worked up about helping them out; it was screwing her son-in-law that made her ecstatically happy. "This will be so-o-o much fun. Tally ho!"

"Wait. You calling us whores?" Ginger hesitated.

"No, Ginger," Dolly informed her. "That's a phrase used when people go hunting, I think."

"Fox hunting." Annie hollered over her shoulder, on her way into her bedroom to change her dress.

Now here they were hours later after an afternoon of Herculean shopping, sitting in the hot tub in their new Caprí swimsuits. And Annie was bawling like an abandoned baby. The other three didn't know quite what to do, other than drink more wine.

Dolly nervously fondled her new diamond stud earrings, which were the size of molars. Maybe this all hadn't been such a good idea. Sure, she loved her new designer clothes and leather luggage and exquisite jewelry, but how legal had this been? In the initial thrill of it all, during the high of shopping like she hadn't shopped since she'd been a star, she hadn't considered the legal ramifications. It had seemed like Annie knew what she was doing. But now that the diva had dissolved into drivel, it had become clear the woman was completely unglued. It was like watching a wax doll melt in the heat.

"And then Pookie died and everything in my life went to shi-i-it." Annie guzzled her wine, drinking in tears along with it.

"How old was Poo … What was his name? I forget." Merry poured Annie more wine. They were on their third bottle. They'd need another soon.

"Whose name?" Annie's eyes skittered. She wasn't sure who'd spoken.

"Your pookie's."

"Oh, him. Um. His name was… Oh, yeah. It was Lemuel Jones. Other people called him Lem. Or Mr. Jones. Or Shithead. But to me, he was always Pookie." Her gaze veered away in memory.

"How old was he when he died? I mean, I remember thinking he was a lot older when you married him about thirty years ago." Ginger recalled the time when Annie had quit burlesque to marry a filthy rich man, many a dancer's dream. Some of them merely got stuck with filthy men. "He must have lived to a ripe old age if he died a few months ago."

Annie managed to focus on Ginger, even though her head bobbed from side to side like a bobblehead doll. "He was 102. I was 32 when we got married. He was 70. Everybody said I was crazy. But that bank account! There was nothing crazy about that." She snorted at the thought. "'Course, I never expected him to live so long. But that was okay. He always treated me like a princess. A queen. No, goddess of the universe." Her giggle terminated in a belch.

"So you two really cared for each other?" Merry asked. "I always assumed you married him for the money."

"Oh, I did. And he knew it. It was our joke. I married him for his money, and he made me earn every penny of it. Ha. We didn't mind. We had fun."

"What kind of fun?" Dolly felt uneasy about taking advantage of Annie's inebriated state but had been mulling over the idea of asking her to participate in their tell-all book. They hadn't told her about it yet. They held off when the shopping began, whispering in-between racks of clothes about loading up and then selling everything on the black market to get the cash for a private dick. As much as that idea appealed to them, they couldn't quite figure out how to get it done. None of them knew where, exactly, the black market was. They'd agreed to talk about it later. In the meantime, they wanted to keep their stuff. They hadn't had any stuff in years.

As for the book, earlier Dolly had taken a break at the mall and found a payphone to call Charlie, the publisher, to tell him where they were staying. He was sending the ghostwriter the very next day. They had to find more dames to contribute, pronto.

Annie mulled over Dolly's question about fun. "Well, we had a lot of sex fun."

That did it. Dolly looked at her two friends and they nodded, so she finally extended the invitation. She explained the book project, concluding with, "We'll each get a thousand-dollar advance, which we can use to hire a private eye to find Balls."

Annie's swollen eyes widened in wonder. She patted her damp hair. A warped smile lined her streaked and splotchy face. "Well, that won't be nearly enough to pay off my mean old lawyer." She hiccupped and took a sip of wine. "But if it helps find Balls so I can get my money, I'm in. You see, I don't really have a retirement fund with him. I loaned him $150,000 last year. I hadn't heard from him in years and got a call out of nowhere. He needed money, so I gave it to him."

"Wait. You did it to piss off your stepson. Right?" Ginger quickly put it all together.

"Sure. But now I need the money back to pay my lawyer. So I'm in on the book. And we get to talk about sex?" Her voice rose to a fevered shrill as she set down her wineglass and clapped her hands. "Yay! That's my favorite subject. I can't wait."

Dolly squirmed under the onslaught of Annie's enthusiasm,

fearing she'd just asked for big trouble, like inviting a grizzly bear over for dinner and then expecting to teach it table manners. But, alas, the deed was done. They now had four former exotic dancers to contribute to their sexy tell-all book.

God help them.

CHAPTER 4

$\mathscr{A}$ racket out in the living room woke Dolly up, and she wasn't happy about it.

"What in hell is that?" Prying her eyes open, the voice that asked the question came out raspy and harsh. She put a palm to her forehead, unable to remember the last time she drank so much wine it gave her a hangover.

The racket would not relent. Not too loud, but incessant. The phone, she realized, the fancy one on the wall that went straight to hotel services. Punch different numbers for different services like food, maid, bellman, front desk, laundry, and car valet. Every room in the penthouse had a phone on the wall, even the bathrooms, but she recalled being told by the bellman that the ringers had been turned off on all of them except the one in the living room, so guests wouldn't be "awoken" should they get a call while sleeping.

"Well, crap. I am awoken. I'm coming, I'm coming." She crawled out of bed and looked down at her new pajamas. They were beautiful. Her skin itself felt like silk under the silk fabric. Deciding that she didn't need a robe, seeing that the PJs covered her whole body, she slipped her feet into her fluffy new slippers, and went to her bedroom door. Before opening it, though, she looked back in wonder at the fabulous room with its pink Italianate décor. She could get used to living like this. At least for the time being, until they got kicked out.

Out in the living room, she answered the phone to have a clerk from the front desk inform her that one James Harrington from Champ Enterprises was there asking to be admitted to the penthouse for a meeting. "Shall I give him a key to the private elevator?"

She had to force her brain to wake up, a feat like trying to untangle a clump of Christmas tree lights. Harrington? Never heard of him. Champ Enterprises? Oh yeah, Champ. Charlie their book publisher.

"What time is it?" she asked, trying to get perspective.

"It's eight o'clock, ma'am."

Beyond the wall of windows bright sunlight shone. It must be a.m. rather than p.m. What was this Harrington guy doing here so early? Realizing that wasn't the desk clerk's problem, she said, "Yeah. Let him up."

Coffee. The elixir of life. That would revive her. The kitchen, which was part of one giant space along with the living room and dining room, had a magic machine that made different kinds of coffee. She needed a big one, straight up. She'd only taken the first few gulps when the elevator chimed, and its doors silently slid open. That was quick.

She turned to see a hobo step out of the contraption.

He looked around. Spying her, he nodded. "Hello, Ms. O'Dare. I'm James." Without further ado, he walked right into the middle of the vast room.

Cheeky, Dolly thought. Maybe a good thing. Maybe bad.

He was old. That didn't bother her – she was getting there herself – she simply hadn't expected it. He was a white man with a swarthy complexion, as if he spent a lot of time outdoors. With unruly white hair, a bushy mustache, a wiry frame, wire-rimmed glasses, faded jeans, a Detroit Tigers tee shirt, scruffy sneakers, a ratty backpack, and an antique duffel bag, her first impression had been a hobo. But now she could see he was simply an old hippie.

She had an urge to flash him the peace sign, but instead set down her coffee mug and went over to shake his hand. The way he homed in on her face, as if she were the only person alive, gave her an unexpected thrill. Strangers didn't look at other people that way these days. They were too distracted. She liked his pale blue eyes.

"This is quite the place," he said as he turned his attention to the view of the famous Vegas strip out the windows. "Ah, I see why you're the only one up." He guffawed, pointing at the four empty wine bottles and dirty wine glasses sitting by the hot tub on the balcony. Damp towels formed piles on the floor. Snack dishes and utensils were scattered about willy-nilly.

Suddenly uncomfortable in her jammies, Dolly said, "Um, how about if you sit over there and make yourself comfortable. I'll be right back." She pointed to the enormous L-shaped sofa and high-tailed it out of there.

The first thing she did back in her bedroom was call maid service to clean up the balcony. Memories of the weird night before needed to be eliminated. Annie's breakdown had been excruciating for all.

Back in the living room after tossing water on her face, brushing her teeth, running a comb through her hair, and throwing on a new pair of jeans and a silk blouse, she was surprised to find this James already set up for work.

"My, aren't you efficient," she noted, referring to the recorder in the middle of the coffee table, the notebook on his lap, and the pen in his hand. His backpack sat open beside him, and she could see it was filled with papers.

"Yes, Ms. O'Dare. No time to lose."

"James, please call me Dolly. I'm wondering how you got here so fast. I thought Charlie was sending someone today, which would mean flying from Detroit to Vegas today."

"Red-eye flight. Love them."

"I see. Would you like coffee? I sure do need some."

"Yes, thank you. Black, please."

In the kitchen, she finished chugging her mugful, quickly made two more cups, and rejoined their ghostwriter.

James held his mug up to blow on the hot, savory brew. After three sips, he set it down, ready to go to work again. Dolly thought maybe he wasn't as Zen as he appeared.

"Do you think the other ladies will be up soon?" he asked.

"I don't know. Maybe. I have a couple of questions first."

He pulled his spectacles down on his nose and looked at her over the rim. Those blue eyes of his unsettled her. She fidgeted in discomfort.

"Making sure I'm legit?"

"No, of course not. I mean, well, yes, I suppose so. Have you written many other books for Champ Enterprises?"

He shoved his glasses back in place. "I've worked for Charlie for thirty-five years, ever since retiring from the Navy." She'd noticed the half-hidden tattoo on his bicep and hadn't quite discerned what it was. Now she could see it was an anchor with rope twisted around it. "I can't even tell you how many screenplays I've written. Books, magazine articles. Hundreds."

"I see. I'm only asking because I don't think our book will be too pornographic, except for this one woman. She's a bit off the charts."

"I assure you, there is nothing she can say that will surprise me or embarrass me in any way. No need for you to be embarrassed, either."

"Oh, I don't expect anything embarrasses you at this point. Me, either. But, you see, Ginger and Merry and I formed such a close friendship, way back in the day, because we were serious about dancing. We worked hard at being professional performers. Not all dancers were like that. Annie, especially, wasn't like that. Oh, don't get me wrong, she was a good dancer, but she was… let's say 'loose' compared to us. There were both kinds of dancers. Some who saw performing and entertaining people as their primary reason for being there and some who saw it as no more than an opportunity to make money off men. Do you get my drift?"

"Sure. Some were prostitutes on the side. Correct?"

"Um, yeah. I guess I could've just spit it out. Ginger and Merry and I, and lots of others, too, didn't do that, even though people often assumed we did. Not to say we didn't have some wild times when we were single girls because we did, but we didn't sell our bodies."

"Don't worry, Dolly. I promise to write it up tastefully but in a way that will sell. After all these years, I'm an expert at that. Does that work for you? Do I pass?"

"Yes. Thank you. I needed to be sure. My husband and I always enjoyed Charlie's movies. Your movies, I now realize. So that's good." In fact, she and Otis had savored them, going to the Champ Adult Theater in downtown Detroit every Friday night for many years. Champ movies were soft porn with plots, interesting characters, and humor. There was no abuse of women. That was one thing Dolly wouldn't tolerate, no way. Champ films were like Shakespeare compared to primitive stag films. Somehow, though, she didn't want to discuss all that right now. It had been a special thing between her and Otis.

James nodded, getting it that her husband had died and she didn't want to talk about it. He didn't either, abruptly switching subjects. "I heard about your manager absconding with your retirement funds. I understand we need to get this done quickly so you ladies will have some money. How about you and I start as best we can? Then when the others are up, I'll go over all the preliminaries and legalities. Is that okay?"

"One more question. We only have four girls so far. Will that be a problem?"

"I do think we'll need six. But we can finish your stories first and then look for more. Now, can we start?"

"Yeah. Or we could just enjoy our coffee." She took a long sip, raising her eyebrows to prove it was good.

Merry stumbled out of her bedroom. "Where's the coffee? I smell coffee." She looked around, confused; then her eyes landed on James. "Oh. I didn't know we had company." She clutched the top of her negligee, amusing Dolly with her modesty, the same reaction she'd had herself. After all, they'd been professional strippers.

"Merry, this is our ghostwriter, James. James, this is Merry, better known as Sister Merry."

He stood up and nodded. "Hello, Merry. Glad to meet you."

"Um, likewise, I'm sure. I'll be right back."

Merry disappeared. The same scene repeated itself until the whole gang sat on the sofa with coffee mugs in hand.

No one had made an attempt at makeup, except for Annie's jab at lipstick, which looked like a three-year-old had been let loose with a red crayon. Everyone had thrown on new jeans. There was an array of pretty tops. Annie's blouse, however, had been misbuttoned, leaving the collar askew and one side hanging down further than the other. She obviously didn't realize that a thatch of her hair stuck out in the back, like a rooster's coxcomb. Nobody here was about to help her out, the way hens usually did for one another.

Despite being hungover, with her appearance in disarray, Annie's old persona had no trouble reappearing in full force. The domineering Annie Fannie they all knew and didn't love was back. The vulnerable mess she'd been the night before had vanished. She might look like shit but, as usual, she acted like top bitch dog of the dung heap.

Dolly was pleased when James showed a remarkable ability to garner control. Direct, this guy didn't suffer fools.

"I have your contracts here," he said as he passed out copies. "You'll see that everything is in order, as Mr. Champ outlined for you. I'll need your signatures on them before I leave here. I'll have copies made in the hotel office to leave with you. I'll interview you here for three days. It'll take me two weeks to write it up and a couple of formatters a week to get it ready for press. A graphic artist is already working on the cover. Mr. Champ, as I believe you know, owns his own printing press, so this can all happen very quickly."

"James, dear," Annie cooed as she sucked up to him, "when do we get our money?"

"I have the checkbook with me. You'll get them when I'm done interviewing you."

"Can I see mine …"

"No. Now …" He went over the terms of the contract, stated that this would be a hard few days of work, and then showed them a list of topics. How they got into the business. What burlesque was like back then. Famous people they met. Their loves and heartbreaks. And sexual escapades. The things Dolly and her friends had anticipated.

He turned on the recorder and said, "Okay, let's begin. I want to take one question at a time and get all your answers, then the next question, so on and so forth. When we're all done with all the questions, we'll do it again, because you will have had time to think them over. Understood?"

Four heads nodded.

"Okay. Let's start with a brief introduction of each of you."

"I'm Anastasia Jones, better known as Annie Fannie." Annie excitedly bounced on her bum.

"Hold that thought, please." James interrupted her interruption of him. "As I was going to say, I'd like to start with Dolly, the first to get into the business, and then take it in chronological order."

"Oh-h-h." Annie displayed her displeasure with a prodigious pout.

Dolly said, "That will be me, Ginger, Annie, and Merry.

"Good." James nodded for her to begin. "Let's start with stage name, real name, where and when you were born, and where you live now. And what kind of work you do now, if any."

"Okay. I'm Dolly O'Dare. That's my stage name and has been my legal name for a long time, too. Seventy years old, born Dolly Devereaux in 1925. I've lived in Detroit, Michigan, my whole life and always had a home there, even when I was on the road all the time. I'm a retired widow."

Satisfied, James pointed his pen at Ginger.

"I'm Ginger, stage name Ginger Snapper, born Geraldine Finklebinder in Peoria, Illinois, in 1926. I'm sixty-nine years old and have lived in Las Vegas for forty years. I'm a waitress and have a tattoo business on the side. I'm single."

When it came Annie's turn, she stated that her stage name had been Annie Fannie because she danced with fans, and that she'd married a wealthy man and her name became Anastasia Jones. She claimed to have been born Anastasia Ambrose to a wealthy family in Palm Beach, Florida, which already sounded fishy. But when she claimed to have been born in 1935, James cocked an eyebrow and said, "Really? Huh." Without skipping a beat, he went on to Merry.

"Well, that's odd, Annie," Merry said, "because I was born in 1935 and have always known I'm the youngest of us all."

"I have no idea where you got that notion," Annie huffed.

"Probably from reality. Anyway, I was born Mary Ann Yates in Ypsilanti, Michigan. I'm sixty years old. I've lived in Golden, Colorado, for a long time because it was a great place to raise my daughter. I was a single parent. She's grown and gone, and I'm a grandma, but I've stayed in Golden because I love it there. I teach yoga and meditation, and do Reiki healings, too."

While Merry talked, Dolly studied Annie. She was probably sixty-seven or sixty-eight. Maybe even seventy, like Dolly. An aura of haughtiness emanated around the bitch, but still it would be hard to pick up on the fact that she was a pathological liar. Dolly now knew this real-life tell-all book might end up being more fiction than fact.

Oh well, too late now. She'd invited the devil to the party and the devil was intent on partying down. The song "Devil Woman" popped into her head. She didn't remember the name of the singer or all the lyrics, but the tune along with the thought of a devilish woman threatened to haunt her for the rest of the day.

CHAPTER 5

$\mathcal{A}$s luck would have it – or did God have a wicked sense of humor? – "Earth Angel" played on the jukebox when they entered the '50s Diner. Seeing that Dolly had been thinking of Annie as the Devil, this song seemed to taunt her.

After two and a half hours of being interviewed, she, Ginger, and Merry had decided they needed brunch. They wanted to get out of the hotel, so suggested walking down the street to the diner the three of them had enjoyed before.

James hadn't seen a need for a break, but he came along anyway. Annie had been upset at having to walk a couple of blocks and groused about the heat the whole way. The others trotted along in glee at making Annie unhappy.

Once inside, Betty, the ebullient waitress they'd had before, rushed up to them. "I'm so glad to see y'all."

"You have a tiara!" Merry pointed to the shiny little rhinestone crown nestled into Betty's beehive. "I love it."

"I have you to thank fer the suggestion." Betty grinned and tapped the tiara. "Ever'body loves it. Here, sit at this big table so we kin talk. I've got somethin' to tell y'all." She settled them around a six-top, which gave her a chair to sit in, too. After plopping down between Dolly and Merry, she excitedly revealed some news.

"I've been askin' around and have a lead on Balls. Y'all haven't found him yet, have ya?"

"No." Dolly shook her head.

"Well, one of the dancers at the Tropicana who comes in here all the time told me one Balls Benedict is also manager of a friend of her cousin's. That friend is an Elvis impersonator who works at the Flamingo. Thing is, she doesn't know the guy's real name, but there's a convention goin' on right now at the Flamingo, so this Elvis guy will definitely be there. I'm thinkin' maybe he knows where yer con man might be."

"That's great. Thanks so much." Dolly's grin lit up her face.

"Looks like we need to visit the Flamingo this afternoon," Ginger said.

"Thanks for asking around, Betty." Merry smiled up at their new friend.

"Sure. Now, even though I may look like a princess ..." Betty pointed to her tiara "... which I've always figured I was in another life, in this life I'm still a waitress. What kin I git y'all?" She pulled out a little pad of paper from her apron pocket and grabbed the pencil she kept stuck in her beehive. After scribbling their orders, she bopped away to Elvis singing "Hound Dog" on the jukebox.

When the women started buzzing about getting to the Flamingo after they ate, James intervened. "Now there, ladies, hold your horses. I figured we'd be working all day."

"But we need to find Balls." Dolly said it as though he'd lost his marbles.

"If that bastard is still in town, he's not going anywhere anytime soon. We need to get our work done."

The women looked at each other, each hoping somebody else would come up with a brilliant retort. Brilliance proved elusive.

Until Dolly said, "Hey, you brought your backpack, so you have your notes." She pointed to the pack he'd put on the floor beside his chair. "We could work right now. You might have questions about what we told you about getting into burlesque." She alluded to their discussion up to then. "We could get that all clarified. If we do that right now while we eat, can we have a break to go talk to that guy?"

James stroked his mustache as he stared her down. "If I said 'no,' would you stay in?"

"Pfft. No-o-o."

"That's what I thought." He pulled his notes and a pen out of the bag. "Okay, I do have a few questions." He pointed at Dolly. "You said you started dancing professionally when you were 16, 1941. This dance craze you talked about, the Lindy Hop, I'd like more detail about that."

"Oh, that was so much fun. The first time I saw a Lindy Hop performance was in the middle of Woodward Avenue in front of Hudson's department store. That's in Detroit. They were having some kind of special sale, so they had a street celebration. Now, I'd never been able to sit still in school. I always had to be moving. I participated in every sport they'd let me join, softball, basketball, track and field. But when I saw that dancing, I knew that's what I'd been born to do."

1941, Woodward Avenue, Detroit, Michigan

THE SKINNY TEEN couldn't hold still. Her body had a mind of its own, ignoring her brain altogether, which was trying to rein her in. Her mother's words echoed inside her head: "Dolly Devereaux! A lady sits still during church. A lady stands still when observing others. A lady ..." The loud music drove the annoying voice away and Dolly started imitating the moves of the dancers in the street.

Standing at the curb amid a crush of enthusiastic onlookers, she jostled her feet, swayed her hips, and snapped her fingers to the rhythm of the live three-piece band. The dancers were jiving like something she'd never seen. It was jazz and boogie and tap and swing all rolled into one.

Out of nowhere, one of the performers grabbed her hand and pulled her into the mix of movers and shakers, and a wave of electricity ratcheted up her body. Before she knew it, she was following her partner's every move, swirling and turning, letting her full skirt unashamedly billow out. When he flung her around so they were back-to-back, wove his arms through hers, and bent over to lift her feet off the ground, she instinctively kicked her legs straight up into the air with a dramatic flair. The audience's zealous reaction sealed the deal.

This was what she wanted to do for the rest of her life.

LAS VEGAS, 1995

"SO I DANCED with Whitey's Lindy Hoppers for a year, until the company folded when all the boys were drafted to fight in the war. We'd go out a month at a time taking the train or a bus to do a circuit of shows all over the Midwest. Fairs, town events, big store openings, things like that. Almost always outside on the street. Except a few times we did a pre-game show for the Harlem Globetrotters. That was exciting! We'd go home for a week, then hit the road again. I loved the gypsy life. Of course, there was no stripping involved. I got into that when the Hoppers ended."

"Why was it called the Lindy Hop?" James asked as he took notes.

"Charles Lindbergh, hopping over the Atlantic Ocean in his

plane in 1927. He was our superhero. So they named a fancy dance after him."

"Who was this Whitey? Sounds like a white man."

"No, he was a black man who'd been a bouncer at the Savoy Ballroom in Harlem. When he saw how white people flocked to the place to watch black dancers, he saw an opportunity and started the troupe in the late '20s. His name was Herbert White, and he had a white streak in his hair." She pointed to the top of her noggin.

"What did your parents think? You must have quit school."

"Yeah, I was in my junior year when I quit. My parents were furious at first, but they always let me come home in-between road trips. They eventually came to believe I'd get the 'dancing thing' out of my system and come home to settle down. They both worked in the Ford plant and during the war the plant was making airplane parts, Army jeeps, tanks, that sort of thing. They needed workers and hired lots of women because men were in short supply. When the Hoppers ended, my parents wanted me to get a good stable job there. That was never going to happen."

Dolly, Ginger, and Merry all tittered at that, unable to imagine Dolly as a factory worker, tinkering with the same job day after day. That was akin to asking an Olympic athlete to spend the rest of their life sitting around playing Twiddly Stix.

Betty brought their food, scrambled eggs and toast for the three of them, a salad for Annie, and a stack of pancakes for James. He had two fried eggs, hashbrowns, and toast on the side. How he stayed slim as a bean pole, Dolly couldn't imagine.

His questions subsided while he chowed down, but as soon as he swallowed his last syrupy bite, he started in again.

"Ginger, you said you started dancing when you were 19. Did you finish high school?"

"Yeah. I did okay in school. I had friends. But after graduation I didn't know what to do. I didn't have a boyfriend and didn't get married right away like most of my girlfriends. I couldn't get a good job, so finally figured 'why not.' No big decision. I just did it."

"What did your parents think?"

"They weren't happy at first. But when I started sending money home, they were okay with it."

"I see." James nodded at Ginger, then looked at Annie. "You said you started dancing when you were 21. What did you do between high school and then?"

"I, um, don't really recall. I worked in a store, I think. But I wanted to dance. Everybody always told me how beautiful I was and everything."

"What did your rich parents in Palm Beach think about that?"

Dolly almost choked on her mouthful of coffee, the mock in James' voice was so obvious. But Annie missed the mock.

"Oh, ah, they were fine with it, as long as I was happy."

"Wow. How very progressive of them."

A furrow formed between his eyes, one that matched Dolly's as she tried to fathom any possible truth to Annie's story.

"O-k-a-a-ay." James looked to Merry. "And what about you? You said you started dancing when you were 24. What did you do between then and high school?"

It may have seemed like a simple enough question, but Merry's eyes filled with tears. She looked at Dolly, then Ginger. Each friend reached across the table to put a comforting hand on her arm.

Merry used her napkin to swipe at her tears. Taking a deep breath, she lifted her head proudly and looked James straight in the eyes. "Okay, I can finally talk about it. Nobody knows this except for Dolly and Ginger and a few other folks, including my daughter. But I'm not embarrassed anymore. I have nothing to be embarrassed about. I don't care who knows, even her." She nodded her head toward Annie, who feigned surprise at the slight. "I've kept this story hidden inside me for far too long. I was a young woman who fell in love, is all. Unfortunately, I was a nun at the time."

Dolly's heart swelled with pride as Merry told her story. She thought about the first time she'd heard Merry tell that tale forty years earlier. Then, her heart had ached with sadness.

Through the years, though, Merry had turned hardship into happiness. It had been tough going at first, but Merry's strength and resilience had pulled her through.

"I always wanted to be a nun," Merry explained to James. "When I was a kid, other girls would dress-up like princesses. I was always wrapping myself up in a white tablecloth to try to look like a nun.

"I joined the convent when I was 18 and married my Lord Jesus Christ when I was 20. However, when I was 22, I broke that vow when a very handsome, very charming 45-year-old priest lured me into an affair. I was head-over-heels, utterly, totally in love. He convinced me that he had the authority to get God's blessing for our relationship. I wanted so badly to believe him, I let that bull-shit assuage my guilt. He claimed our love fed our souls, which made us better servants of God and our Lord Jesus.

"I fell for his crap like a hypnotized zombie. A combination of naiveté, lack of education, and raging hormones took control of my entire existence – my thoughts, my actions, my beliefs. We would meet in the church cemetery at midnight three nights a week. It sounds gruesome, but I was so in love I found it to be exciting. It felt as if all those old souls were supporting our love affair. He'd always bring a blanket and we'd have sex right there among the tombstones. In fact, our special spot was under the headstone of one Ernest Love. I know, it sounds like a bad joke, but I thought it was a sign of God's blessing. I never considered what poor Ernest might have thought."

Dolly pried her gaze away from her friend and studied James.

He'd stopped taking notes, instead hanging onto Merry's every word.

"When I told him I was pregnant – which was inevitable, by the way, because I knew nothing about birth control – I assumed he'd be happy. I believed with every fiber of my being that he loved me so much he'd be overjoyed at this news. We'd leave the church, marry, raise a family, and find another way to serve God.

"He told me to get an abortion." She paused, needing a deep breath. Fortified, she continued. "There are no words to describe the devastation I felt. It was like being thrust into an alternate universe, like being cast out into space with no lifeline to earth. I couldn't comprehend what he was saying. My brain had no room for that kind of information. Abortion went against everything the church preached, against everything I believed. My body, however, somehow understood. I couldn't breathe. Then it felt as if every bit of energy was sucked out of me through the top of my head. I fainted."

She took a gulp of water and used her napkin to wipe a bead of sweat from her brow.

"When I came to, he was gone. There I was, passed out in the middle of a cemetery in the dark of the night. Pregnant. All by myself. Except for poor Ernest Love. And it was going to stay that way, I realized. I picked myself up, went to my room in the convent, packed my few possessions, and left. I never went back."

She had directed her narrative at James and now looked at Annie to gauge her reaction. Annie, for once, remained mum.

Merry continued. "I knew I couldn't go home to my parents. They would have kicked me out for my wickedness. I ended up waitressing in a burlesque club where, thank God, I had the good fortune to meet Dolly and Ginger. It didn't take them long to figure out I was pregnant. They helped me work right up until my Gracie was born. Then I kept the baby backstage and the dancers would take turns watching her when they weren't on. For some miraculous reason, it worked. Especially when they taught me to dance so I'd make more money.

"That's my story. From nun to stripper. How do you like that?"

James stared at Merry for a few measured moments, taking it all in. "I don't like it at all," he finally said, "that a son-of-a-bitch priest took advantage of you. I do like it that you three women stuck together, and you made a life for yourself and your daughter. I admire you for that. I'm starting to see that this story is about a lot more than just 'exotic dancing.' It's about deep friendship. It's about building a community in even the most unusual of circumstances. It's about a truly special kind of strength and love you women have that we need more of on this planet."

Dolly couldn't help but enjoy James's mushy take on Merry's story. He might actually be an old hippy, after all.

CHAPTER 6

$\mathcal{D}$olly accidentally bumped into Elvis Presley.

"Sorry, love. I didn't mean to be cruel." His Elvis voice was pitch perfect and his white jumpsuit, shiny belt, and purple scarf mimicked the icon in his later years.

He sidled away and she tunked another one.

"It's now or never, darlin'." This one was cuter than the first, but his voice wasn't quite right. And his skinny frame in another version of the white jumpsuit didn't look anything like the heftier guy Elvis became. He winked and moved on.

The lobby and casino of the Flamingo was so crowded with impersonators it was impossible to walk through the mass of bodies without jostling around. There were Elvises as far as the eye could see, mingled in with Liza Minnelli, Bette Davis, Jerry Lee Lewis, Cary Grant, Stevie Wonder, Carmen Miranda, Blaze Starr, and many others. It was impossible to keep up. How she and the girls would ever find the Elvis they needed, she didn't know. But the tableau of characters gave her a thrill. These were performers who loved kitchy costumes. Right up her alley.

"I feel 'All Shook Up'," she told her companions with a chuckle.

Annie ignored her and bulldozed her way up to the hotel registration desk. "I need your help," she demanded.

The desk clerk erased an involuntary grimace and replaced it with a faux smile. "Yes, ma'am. What may I do for you?"

"There's an Elvis impersonator who works here. Which one is he?" She pointed back toward the crowd.

The clerk's upper lip flinched. Dolly figured he probably didn't usually give out that kind of information but knew that if he did, this impudent woman would get out of his frazzled life.

"There's a registration desk for the impersonator conference in front of the showroom." He pointed out across the casino floor. "They will know."

Dolly admired his ability to deflect responsibility.

They trooped across the hotel lobby area, through the casino, and on to the desk for the conference. There they were met by Superman.

"Look! It's a bird, it's a plane … it's Superman!" Merry greeted the man. "I bet you hear that a hundred times a day."

The man jovially put his hands on his hips in the traditional Superman pose. "Yup. And it never gets old. What can I do for you lovely ladies? I must say, you don't need to impersonate anybody. You're the real thing."

As much as she knew that was shtick and he was full of shit, the guy entertained Dolly. She loved the campy mood of this gathering. "We need to know which Elvis is the one who works here."

"Oh, sorry, I'm from Boise, so I don't know. But I know somebody who will know." In a booming voice he shouted at Roy Rogers, who stood talking to a group of chorus girls.

Roy came over, appraised the females in a way that would have made Dale Evans grind her teeth, and pointed out the Flamingo Elvis. They thanked him and Superman and wove their way over to the guy.

Dolly liked this version of the iconic rock-and-roll singer. He was the early Elvis, before the pretentious white jumpsuit, ostentatious belt, and silky scarf. This was the way she first fell in love with the star – tight pants, a button-down shirt open at the collar, and glossy patent leather shoes. Tussled dark hair with sideburns. And a body to drool over. Every teenaged girl and young woman in America would have run away with him, if that gorgeous Priscilla hadn't snagged him first. He'd oozed sexiness, and this impersonator oozed with the best of them.

Once Dolly explained that they were trying to find one Ballard Benedict and why, the man lost his slick Elvis voice and stance, and he shuffled them into an alcove. "I've been looking for that creep for months." His natural voice was huskier than Elvis's ever thought of being. "I don't have a retirement fund with him, and I'm nowhere near retirement anyway, but he owes me for my last four gigs outside the Flamingo. They pay me directly; I'm a full-time performer here. But Balls sets up my outside jobs and he's supposed to pay me. He screwed you ladies, too? Big time, huh? Oh, I'm so sorry. I'll do whatever I can to help find the scumball."

"We appreciate that," Dolly told him. "So you have no idea where he could possibly be right now or how to find someone who might know?"

"I'm afraid not. I wish I did."

"Okay. We know where to find you. If we find him, we'll let you know. And if you find out anything, we're staying in the penthouse at the Bellagio."

He whistled. "Nice going."

"It's a long story."

"I bet. Hey, were the four of you chorus girls or something?"

"Not exactly. We were exotic dancers."

"Strippers." For some reason Dolly didn't understand, Annie felt the need to clarify.

"Wow. Cool." He fell back into his Elvis persona and sang the first few lines of "Can't Help Falling in Love." He was good. Very good. Dolly sort of fell in love all over again. He brought back fond memories of her youth.

They bid him goodbye and wormed their way through the crowd and made it outside before being stopped by Superman.

"Hey, ladies!" His red cape fluttered behind him as he sprinted toward them. "We're doing a show in ten minutes. Why don't you join us? My treat. Front row seats."

"Sure," Annie chirped.

"Sounds great," Merry agreed.

"Why not?" Ginger joined in.

"Why not? Because we need to get back to work." Dolly hated being the bitch slave master, as she'd love nothing more than seeing the show. But she feared James would not only be pissed off but would abandon them altogether if they didn't get back as promised.

Before she could object any further, however, her crew hustled back inside to be swallowed by the tangle of pretenders.

"Shit. We'll be in deep doo-doo now. But what the hell." She dove into the crowd.

"THAT WAS SO-O-O MUCH FUN." Annie had been ooo-ing and ahh-ing about the show to the point that Dolly wanted to strangle her. The woman hadn't shut up all the way back to their temporary home.

Sure, Dolly had loved the show – it had been exciting to watch so much talent with music and dancing and singing and comedy – but once it was over, her mind turned back to their book. She'd been anxious to get back. The show had been two-and-a-half hours long, and then everyone had insisted on drinks. Therefore, they were really, really late. She assumed James hated late.

She felt relieved when the private elevator doors opened to deposit them into the living room, allowing her to hightail it to her bedroom to get away from Annie. She didn't see James as she passed through the main room, so figured he was in his bedroom. He certainly would have heard them clamor in, especially Annie's mind-numbing chatter. He would come out to get to work again.

In her bedroom, Dolly quickly freshened up, finishing by glancing at herself squarely in the mirror. "Okay, get in there and face the music. James will be very unhappy."

But James had not materialized. With fear edging its way into her thoughts, she rapped on his bedroom door. It swung open. James was gone, lock, stock, and barrel. Backpack and duffel bag, too. His room was cleared out and it looked like the maid had already made it up anew.

"Oh no," she whispered. James had abandoned the project because she and this gaggle of girls were too unreliable. They didn't fit his driven work style. Not only was their money from the book gone, but she was also flabbergasted at the depth of her disappointment that James was gone. She liked him more than she wanted to admit.

The others gathered in the living room and Dolly delivered the dire news.

"Crimony, I'm so sorry we annoyed him." Merry shook her head remorsefully. "He's a nice man. It seemed like he really wanted to make our book a hit."

"Well, I think he's being a brat. After all, we only went to a matinee." Annie objected to no one who cared.

"Damn. We need that money. I know! We could call the airport and have him paged. Maybe we can talk him out of leaving." Ginger's suggestion proved a hit, so she went to the phone and started to dial.

They all looked up at the elevator in surprise when it chimed. The doors opened and a beautiful woman stepped out. Maybe 65 years old, Dolly figured, she had a great figure under a flowery sundress. Splendid gray streaks highlighted her lush dark hair. She held herself like royalty, albeit with a fancy cane.

"Layla?" Dolly asked incredulously. "Layla! Is that you?"

"Of course, dear." Even after so many years in the U.S., Layla had a tinge of a charming Middle Eastern accent.

Dolly rushed to her old friend, and they fell into a hug. When Ginger and Merry caught on to the identity of their visitor, they joined in. The four of them clutched onto each other in a huddle like celebrating footballers.

When they finally parted, Dolly asked how Layla came to be there.

"Him," Layla said, nodding toward James, who'd come out of the elevator behind her. He pulled a decidedly feminine pink roller bag. A young woman stood beside him, her own pink roller bag in tow.

Dolly turned to James. "I'm so glad to see you. I was afraid we totally pissed you off when we didn't come back like we said we would."

James shook his head. "Well, I always like to get the job done, but I'm too old to get pissed off too easily or too often." He turned his attention to Layla. "I'll put your bag in your room." Looking back at Dolly, he explained. "I moved out and had my room cleaned up for Layla and Malika, so you girls can all stay together. I got a room a few floors down, not too far away. You can't get rid of me that easily." He grinned, allowing Dolly to enjoy the lines that gathered along his cheeks. Then he turned and took the bag into the bedroom.

"How on earth did he find you?" "Where do you live?" "Are you here in Vegas?" "Is this your granddaughter?" "She must be. She looks just like you." In the excitement, questions were thrown at Layla like darts.

Layla laughed and said, "Wait, wait. We'll get to all of that. But first, yes, this is my granddaughter, Malika. Malika, these are the friends I've told you about so many times."

The stunning young woman embraced each of her elders, calling each by name. She even included Annie, who hadn't participated in the merriment to this point. Dolly immediately liked the girl for her inclusive generosity, even if it was with Annie.

Malika took her bag into the bedroom she'd share with her grandmother. Thankfully, that room had two full sized beds. She and James returned to the living room, so Dolly suggested they all get something to drink and sit down to catch up. Once everybody had a glass of water, bottle of beer, glass of wine, or bottle of soda pop in hand, they settled into the L-shaped sofa.

"When my interviewees didn't return this afternoon," James explained, clearing his throat to make fun of them, "I did a little investigative work. The concierge found me an old phone book, and lo and behold Ballard Benedict's talent agency was listed in the yellow pages. I'd heard his name but didn't know where his office was. Once I had the address, I took a cab to the building. An accountant in the office next to his was most willing to spill the beans about his former neighbor. He didn't know where Mister Benedict had gone, but he did have the number of a woman and her granddaughter who'd been there looking for him."

"Yes," Layla interjected. "That nice accountant said he'd call me if Balls showed up. You see, Malika and I moved here a few months ago for her job as an event planner. We're right here in Vegas."

"So, Balls stole your money, too." Dolly said it as a statement, not needing to ask.

"Yes, I'm afraid so."

"When I called Layla," James continued, "and told her about the book, she was immediately all in. I knew you'd like to have her stay here. Besides, I thought it'd be a nice surprise."

"It is. It's wonderful," Dolly reassured him. Ginger and Merry heartily agreed.

James then asked Layla the same questions he'd asked the others so far. Her answers revealed that she was born in Baghdad, Iraq, and came to the U.S. to attend college. When she fell in love with an American salesman, her wealthy parents disowned her. She'd understood that her parents wanted her to get an education and come home to marry an "appropriate," successful Iraqi man. But their rejection crushed her at the time. Had it not been for the surreptitious financial support of her loving brothers back home, she would have been penniless and unable to finish college. The salesman, however, swooped in to marry her, she finished a degree in literature, they had four children, and then he died unexpectedly of a massive heart attack before their last infant sprouted his first tooth. Life came crashing down on her. There was some insurance money but not enough. She needed to make a living.

"The one thing I was really good at," Layla explained, "was belly dancing. I grew up in a privileged home; my parents were very rich. But my brothers and I always enjoyed being around the servants more than our mother and father. They were – shall I we say – stuffy. The maids and our nanny used to entertain us kids by dancing. It was a big secret, though. Belly dancing was considered crass by the upper crust. We never told. That way we got to have fun. The boys learned to play doumbek drums. I learned to dance to the beat of the music.

"At first, it was a kid-friendly version, of course. But by the time I was 13, my nanny was taking me to performances she did at a club on weekends. I was smitten. That was what I wanted to do. When I came to the states, though, I didn't know what to do with the one talent I possessed. However, when I had to quickly figure out how to make a living, I found clubs that hired dancers. Mediterranean and Greek restaurants, supper clubs, burlesque theaters. My stage name was Lovely Layla. The rest is history."

"Couldn't your brothers help you out financially after your husband died?" James asked the question that had always been on Dolly's mind.

"They would have, but there was a change in regimes and therefore in my family's financial situation. By then they were as broke as I was. They tried to come over here so we could all help each other out, but that never worked out, either. I've never seen them again." A veil of sadness cloaked her voice.

"What she isn't telling you," Malika interjected, "is that she's the most amazing woman alive and did what she had to do to raise her family. And everybody is doing great. My mom is happy and healthy in Florida, my aunt and uncles are thriving, and I have lots of cousins. She built a wonderful life for us."

Layla smiled and patted her granddaughter's knee. "I am one lucky woman. But, James, I know you want to know about the dancing. Well, my parents would have been appalled. If I hadn't already been thrown out of the family, they would have done it had they ever known that I got up on stage in a skimpy costume and rolled my hips to make a living." She tittered. "And I loved it."

"She was incredible," Dolly told James. "You were one of the best dancers I'd ever seen," she reassured Layla. Looking back at James, she said, "She worked steadily at those places in Chicago, where she lived, and that's where we met her."

"Yes," Layla added, "I had to stay close to home because I had a family. I didn't travel around like these girls."

"You see," Dolly explained, "the way Ginger, Annie, and I worked was to travel all the time. Balls would book us and others, like the bands and singers and comedians, at different venues all over the place."

"Except Annie and I stayed in the states," Ginger explained, "while Dolly ended up going all over the world, she was so popular."

"And I stayed as close to Colorado as possible because of my daughter," Merry said. "I traveled some and took her when she was little but once she was school age, I seldom went anyplace where I'd have to stay overnight. I met Dolly and Ginger when they had a gig for the summer at a house of burlesque near where I lived, when I was still waitressing there. They came back almost every summer. And later Annie came there, too."

"But those of us who travelled all the time, Dolly and Annie and I, didn't always work together. It didn't work like that," Ginger explained. "We had no control over our schedules. Balls would book whatever the client wanted. One dancer. Two. Five. A band or not. A singer or comedian. Like that. Sometimes we worked alone and sometimes with a few of us and sometimes with the whole crew. A week was the minimum, but it was usually at least two weeks."

"So we didn't get to see each other often, but it was sheer delight when we did." Dolly hoisted her glass in a salute to her friends. "Layla's belly dance routine was so different from ours, it was a delight when we got to see it."

"Well, girls, I must tell you" Layla patted her granddaughter's shoulder "… Malika can dance like something you've never seen. It's called tribal fusion now, and she's the best."

"If you taught her, I'm sure she's as good as you were," Dolly said.

"No. She's better."

"Oh, grandma, you're prejudiced." Malika's long, thick hair fell over her shoulder in a soft wave as she shook her head. Dolly remembered Layla's hair once being the exact same hue of deep brown, like fertile earth. The young woman was so beautiful Dolly wondered if an audience would even care if she could dance. Layla had been the same, and she could dance. It warmed Dolly's heart to see that gift being passed down.

Malika went into the bedroom to retrieve her grandmother's scrapbook to add to the collection on the coffee table and the rest of the evening was spent scouring through each other's mementoes. They ordered room service for dinner. Lots of giggling ensued, with a tear here and there, as well. Even Annie eventually got into the swing of things and laughed at some of the photos. She was in Merry's scrapbook, big feathery fans and all.

Dolly noticed James quietly sitting back, taking it all in. He seemed content. Every now and then he'd jot down notes. When everyone finally retired for the evening, she came back out of her bedroom to find James going through the scrapbooks, putting cocktail napkins in-between some of the pages.

"Are those the pages that have photos you want for the book?"

He looked up and didn't answer, instead gazing at her in a way that heated her entire body as if she'd stepped into a sultry tropical night. She hadn't felt like this since being with her husband Otis and wasn't sure what she thought about it. She'd changed into a pair of silk pajamas, this time demurely covered by a matching silk robe.

Finally, he said, "Oh, yeah. Good observation."

He didn't look away.

She didn't, either.

"Do you mind if I ask you some questions about your life?" she asked. "After all, it only seems fair. You know a lot about us and are about to know more."

"Ask away and I'll decide if I want to answer." That smile again, the one that caused a crease to shoot up each of his cheeks. She supposed they'd been mere dimples when he was younger. Now they were magnets pulling in a woman's lips.

She sat down beside him. "Are you married? I mean, I've wondered, if you are, what your wife thinks of your career and your being here with us."

He took a long draw on his bottle of Coke as he mulled over his answer. "I've been married twice, the first time when I was a clueless kid at U of M, and I got a girl I barely knew pregnant. She divorced me when I got drafted for World War II. A real 'Stand by Your Man' kind of gal." He scoffed. "We have one son, who I adore. I have three grandchildren and a great-grandchild, all in Michigan. I liked the Navy well enough that when the war ended, I made it a career for twenty years. I married a Hawaiian woman along the way. But she wasn't about to move from sunny Hawaii back to temperamental Michigan. I didn't want to be anywhere else; so that marriage didn't last, either. You see, I'd missed so much of my son's life when he was young because I was at sea so often. Once that was over I wanted to be near him. And he wanted that, too."

"That's when you started working for Charlie Champ?"

"Yes. Charlie and I have been buddies since we were kids. We grew up on the same block in Hamtramck."

"Ah, I know it well. I grew up on the east side of Detroit, of course." Dolly knew that being a native Detroiter, James understood that the Black neighborhoods were east of the city. "Did you have any writing experience when you started with Charlie?"

"Sort of. For a year after the Navy, I tried to become the next Ernest Hemingway. When that didn't work out, Charlie saved my ass by hiring me. To my surprise, I discovered I have a knack for writing soft porn and have been doing it ever since. My son was old enough to know about it by the time I started, but we have an agreement that young family members don't need to know until they're twenty-one. So far, nobody has accused me of being a depraved reprobate, so we're doing okay."

"It's really worked out for you."

"Yes, it has. I've been extremely fortunate."

Dolly looked out the window at the bright lights of the Las Vegas night, contemplating fortune. "I feel the same way. I loved being a dancer."

James took the final gulp of his soda, which opened the door for her next question. She pointed to his empty bottle. "I've noticed you don't drink alcohol."

"Nope. Not for twenty-five years, ever since my last bar brawl resulted in a broken nose and two broken ribs. I'd finally had enough of having my body pummeled for reasons my inebriated brain couldn't remember."

"I see. Did you ever do any pummeling in return?"

"Oh yeah. That got old, too. I never let my drinking interfere with my work, but the minute I had a night off, I always seemed to end up in the emergency room or the clink."

"Does it bother you to be around people who drink? Like here with us?"

"Not at all. I gave up smoking at the same time I gave up booze, and if I were to fall off the wagon it would be for a coffin nail, not hooch."

"I gave up smoking years ago, too. That is tough."

That stare again with those blue eyes. Her innards stirred. She popped up off the couch.

"Well, I guess it's time to hit the rack," she announced.

James slowly stood up, took his pop bottle to the kitchen, tossed it in the recyclable bin, came back to pick up his backpack, and strode toward the elevator. He turned around and threw her a cockeyed grin. "I'll see you in the morning, Dolly."

"Yeah. See you then." She struggled to sound nonchalant.

As soon as the elevator doors closed with James behind them, her knees almost gave way. "Holy shit, I like him. I feel like a 14-year-old girl with my first crush." Her adult wrangled control and said, "Oh, stop it, Dolly. He might only want to be friends. Behave yourself." But her rebellious 14-year-old self said, "Nope. No way."

Dolly O'Dare went to bed as confused as she'd been that night so many years ago when she'd actually been 14 and Bobby Smithers wanted to kiss her on their first date. She hadn't known what to do. Bobby solved the problem by smacking her square on the lips. And that had been the start of it all.

CHAPTER 7

"I mean, so many of us performers and other workers were young, and we had big dreams and energy galore, and our hormones were boiling out of control. Plus, we were on the cusp of understanding these great new adult bodies we had. There were a lot of drop-dead gorgeous people. So of course, there was some sex going on."

Dolly had answered James' question about her first job as an exotic dancer. She'd considered not being truthful, so as not to frighten off her crush, but berated herself for being silly. The man wrote porn. He would not be driven away by sex.

There was more to the story. "The owners of the place were upstanding citizens, and lots of famous people owned land and cottages there. Even W.E.B. DuBois, the famous writer and civil rights leader. The owners did everything in their power to keep us workers on the straight and narrow. But like most young people, we found a way."

It was early morning and the whole gang was gathered on the couch with enough donuts and coffee to wake the dead. Dolly had explained that after Whitey's Lindy Hoppers, her first jobs were in random Detroit clubs and then at Idlewild, an African American resort community in the western part of the lower peninsula of Michigan. Easily accessible from Chicago and Detroit, the resort had been founded in the 1920s by black entrepreneurs who wanted to provide vacation facilities for people who were unable to enjoy such places in the white world. Known as the Black Eden, it had restaurants, night clubs, a lake, and entertainment so spectacular that many a night there were as many white people in the audience as blacks.

"At first, I was a chorus girl but quickly got promoted to a solo spot. The Paradise Club where I worked didn't have a big razzle dazzle Las-Vegas-type show yet. That came a few years later, when Arthur Braggs took over to produce the shows and they became really spectacular. There were acts like The Four Tops, Sarah Vaughn, Cab Calloway, Louis Armstrong." She paused, trying to picture all of them. "Let's see, oh, Dinah Washington, Aretha Franklin, Fats Walker. So many, it's impossible to remember all of them. B.B. King, he was one of my favorites. Arthur had the Idlewild Review, too, a group of us dancers he sent out to perform in other places in the winter, when Idlewild clubs were closed. He even booked me at the Apollo Theatre once in Harlem. That was a dream come true.

"But that all started in 1950, about five years after I started at Idlewild. In the beginning, there were live bands, singers, comedians, and only a few showgirls. I admit, I was nothing to write home about at first, but they didn't fire me and I got better. By the time Arthur came along, I was ready. That's when I became a star."

"What about the sex thing? Get back to that." Annie wasn't at all interested in hearing about the development of Dolly's career. She wanted the salacious details about her sex life.

Dolly surprised herself by answering. "Well, I admit I had a hard time choosing one young man to fall for. There were so many. And so many of those were hunks." She chuckled while

Annie nodded approval. "I was young, single, and responsibly using birth control, a diaphragm. Somehow the whole thing about getting married and having children had totally eluded me, despite being raised Catholic and being Catholic to this day. At least I was honest with myself about that and didn't try to squeeze myself into a life that wasn't for me. If I hadn't loved to dance so much, I might have done that because of pressure from my family and from society in general. But I had to dance, so that was that."

"So you had a lot of lovers." Annie wouldn't relent.

"I had my share. I confess, I liked having sex and my morals were a little loose back then."

"You mean your vagina was a little loose." Annie was the only one who laughed at her own joke.

Dolly let it pass. Annie was starting to become like background noise to her, not worth getting emotional about. Besides, this time the damned dame was right.

IDLEWILD, Michigan, 1945

STANDING BACKSTAGE, Dolly hoisted up the bustier of her costume to give herself as much cleavage as possible. The costume designer had done a fabulous job on this one with its built-in push-up bra, cinched-in waist, and mermaid skirt. The whole shebang was covered in shiny lavender material with sequins bordering the top and bottom. Best of all, the zipper on the side was guaranteed not to get stuck like the one last time.

The comedian on stage finished his routine to rousing applause. The band played his exit music and then switched to her entrance song. It was a great band, playing R&B and jazz to perfection. Dolly strutted out to the rhythm of the strident beat. The audience cheered. She threw up her arms and tossed out a big smile. They cheered even more. And then it began, the seductive swaying of her hips, the twisting of her shoulders, the gliding of her feet across the floor. By the time she unzipped the sexy dress, the audience was going wild.

There were a lot of soldiers there on this night, home from that wretched war that had ended only weeks earlier. Many were still in uniform. There was one at a table in the front row who caught her eye as he eyed her up and down. Square jaw. Blond hair. Raw sensuality. A uniform that hid a tall frame on what promised to be a delicious naked body.

She held up her unzipped dress, turned her back to the audience, waited several beats, and then let the garment cascade to the floor around her feet, thereby allowing her admirers to revel in the pleasure of ogling her toned backside from top to bottom. Her buttocks were, of course, covered by little panties, which the costumer had thoughtfully sequined to match her dress.

Dolly continued to move to the music as the crowd cheered, never turning back toward them. She ran her hands through her long hair and lifted it up to expose the back of her pretty neck. Yes, she knew that was like a wild animal submitting to its dominant partner. But, she wondered, who was truly the dominant one in such a mating ritual?

Looking over her shoulder, she was disappointed to see that the handsome blond soldier's chair sat empty.

The music ended with a crescendo and Dolly trotted off stage, sticking her arm out to wave to the audience from behind the side curtain. She might be quite new at this but couldn't imagine that the thrill of applause would ever get old. They clapped and hooted and hollered and whistled. She loved it.

"Dolly. Hey. You were great. Again. Gee. It sure is fun to watch you dance."

She grabbed the beach towel she always had ready off stage to wrap around her nearly naked body. A lighting guy had snuck up beside her while she covered herself.

"Oh, Claude. Hi. Thanks."

As they talked, the band struck up another song while the stage curtain went down and a couple of stagehands set up the next act, a singing duo. One of the stagehands brought over her dress.

"Thanks." She draped the costume over a stool. The stagehand swiftly hurried away, and she figured she knew why. He'd been at the party in the woods the weekend before when Dolly and Claude had been making out. The guy, she knew, was giving Claude another opportunity to hit on her.

Claude was cute, that she had to admit. A bit puny, maybe, but not bad. Her own body tingled from the excitement of having performed. A warm sheen covered her skin. Her desires screamed at her to give Claude what he so clearly wanted.

They kissed. Then again. He took her hand and led her to a small prop room a few feet away. Once inside, he attempted to close the door, but it wouldn't latch. They didn't care. Their bodies melded together. The towel fell off. His hands roamed all over her. She lost all control. Until the critical moment came.

"Wait. No, stop. Wait, I said." She swatted his hands away. "Where's the rubber? I told you I don't wear the spongy thing when I dance and that you'd always need to have a rubber handy."

"Oh. I forgot." He dove in for another kiss.

She patted his cheek and shoved his face sideways. "No. I told you, not without protection."

"Oh, come on," he groaned. "Don't be a bitch."

"Bitch? Bitch, huh. No, I'm just not a flaming idiot, which you obviously are." She pushed him away from her, and he tumbled out the door.

Picking himself up off the floor, he growled, "Bitch," and scampered away.

Dolly picked up her towel, wrapped it around herself, and peeked out the door. Lo and behold, there stood the handsome blond soldier, nonchalantly leaning against the wall. He straightened up, put a hand in his pocket, and came out with a teensy-tiny package. Clinching it between his index and middle fingers, he held it up for her to witness.

Dolly looked from the blue Trojan package into his blue eyes and back at the package. Snatching it out of his hand, she backed into the prop room. The handsome blond soldier followed and had no trouble latching and locking the door behind him.

The immediate press of their bodies felt like two long-lost lovers coming together after a painful parting. Suddenly, though, the soldier pulled back, his hands resting on her hips. He heart sunk. Her confidence evaporated. Maybe he didn't like her.

But then he tugged off her towel, plucked off her pasties, and slipped off her panties. She stood in front of him buck naked, watching as his eyes roved up and down her body and alit with pleasure. Her confidence soared.

Her lips parted.

His lips covered them.

Then it was her turn. She pushed him back, arms' length away. He dipped his chin and gazed down at her, knowing what was coming.

Following his lead, she undressed him slowly, methodically exposing what turned out to be a sublime specimen of a male body. Running her hands down his chest, she found a thick scar. He'd been wounded in battle. Thank God those foreign fuckers hadn't killed him.

As important as the rubber had been to her, she'd forgotten about it. He did not forget, picking it up off the table beside them where she'd dropped it. He expertly unrolled it into place.

Their lovemaking began deliberately, masterfully, as he worked his way around her body, kneading her flesh here and there until it thrilled her everywhere. She'd never experienced anything like it.

The few boys she'd been with were grabby and needy. This was no boy. This was a man who knew how to make love to a woman, teaching her how to reciprocate.

She gave it all she had.

When he reached around to cup her butt in his hands, lift her up to sit on the table, and enter her, she thought she might die of sheer ecstasy right then and there. It would be worth it.

It was then that their coupling became desperate, her legs cinched around his hips, clasping with each thrust. At the precise same moment, he groaned and she yelped as they shared the ultimate primitive pleasure.

To her delight, he didn't withdraw, dress, and dash away like boys did. He took his time, holding her head in his hands and showering her face with kisses as light as butterfly wings. When their bodies parted, he picked up the towel and handed it to her. As she wrapped herself in the towel, she watched as he detached his rubber, tied the end like a balloon, and tossed it into a nearby waste can.

She offered the edge of her towel, and he took it to wipe himself off. He dressed, making sure his uniform was well in place, looked around, found what he wanted, and picked up her pasties and panties. When he offered them to her, she kept the pasties but stuffed the panties into his pocket. He nodded knowingly, acknowledging the secret bond they would forever share. With that, he left.

Dolly stood stone still for several minutes.

They had never spoken.

She didn't even know his name.

And she never saw him again.

1995, Las Vegas

. . .

A WARM SHIVER slithered through Dolly's body at the memory of the explosive romp way back when. Annie had been blathering as Dolly so salaciously daydreamed, but she forced herself to tune in again. She was about to say something else about Idlewild when the phone rang. Ginger got up to answer.

"Ah ha …. Ah ha …. Okay …. Sure. Let them up." She hung up, twirled around, and did a little jig. "Elvis and Superman are here. They think they might know where to find Balls."

"Wow. How nice of them to come over." Merry was delighted.

Dolly considered that. "Hmmm. Seems like they could have called to tell us what they know. I'm guessing they just want to see the Bellagio penthouse."

"Elvis?" Layla queried.

"And Superman?" Malika inquired.

James said, "Don't worry, you get used to strange things happening with this bunch."

Ginger offered to refresh everyone's beverages while they waited. She finished playing waitress and sat back down when the elevator chimed, the doors slid open, and two hunks stepped into the room. Gaping stares by the females greeted them.

Dolly recognized who was who first. The sideburns gave Elvis away. "Wow. We didn't recognize you in street clothes. Come in, come in." She popped up, motioned them into the room, and made introductions all around. Everyone stood and James shook hands with them.

Elvis' real name was Rhett Cutler. Not quite *Gone with the Wind*, Dolly thought, but close enough.

When the man who impersonated Superman introduced himself as Clark Kent, they all laughed until he reassured them that was his real name. His Kent parents had their first date at a Superman movie.

"And here I am as a result." He playfully twirled his hand from head to toe. "In the flesh."

Both men's line of sight glommed onto Malika as she sat back down. Dolly recognized the male peacock strut, the puffing out of the chest and raising of the chin. Ah, those young hormones she'd been talking and daydreaming about. They gave it away every time, sending signals like a neon sign. Malika didn't seem to object as she crossed her perfectly sculpted legs and pulled her skirt up an inch to show more thigh above the knee.

The ladies and James sat back down, but the two visitors demurred.

Suddenly seeming to remember his reason for being there, Elvis – Dolly would always think of him that way rather than by his real name – pried his eyes away from Malika's gams and said, "We don't have much time. We're on at the convention in an hour, so we barely had enough time to come over and let you know we ran into somebody who might know where Balls is at. Here." He burrowed into his jeans pocket, came up with a scrap of paper, and handed it over to Dolly. She glanced at it to see the name and address of a two-bit motel outside of town. "A guy thinks he saw him over there, staying in one of the rooms on the bottom floor, on the east end. He isn't sure it was Balls, but he used to know him years ago and thinks this older guy is him."

"Let's go." Ginger stood up like a battle commander. "I'll go get the equipment." She rushed into her room and came back out with a small box. She stuck it in her purse, which sat on a table with all the purses by the elevator door.

Annie had already gone to the elevator and pushed the down button.

Dolly was halfway to the elevator herself before she remembered to turn back to the others. "Oh, Rhett, Clark," she said, forcing herself to remember their names, "thank you so much. We owe you one. Layla, do you want to come?"

"No, dear, I'm too slow with this cane. Go get him for all of us."

"James," Dolly said, "I hope you don't mind." She pointed to the elevator, its doors already open with Ginger, Merry, and Annie barreling inside. "Okay?"

He nodded, conceding defeat.

As the doors closed, Dolly caught a glimpse of Elvis and Superman sitting down on either side of Malika. So much for being in a hurry to get back to the convention. Hormones ruled.

<h1 style="text-align:center">CHAPTER 8</h1>

"Over there. That end." Ginger pointed at the far end of the shabby one-story motel.

"No, no. This end right here," Annie insisted, pointing at the closest end.

"No, he said east end. That's east." Ginger's impatience glowered.

"No, this is east."

Annie, who was driving her Bentley, pulled in where she wanted.

"U-u-ugh," Ginger groaned. "Now we have to walk down there."

"No, we don't. It's here."

Dolly had tuned out of the navigation bickering. Obviously, allowing Ginger and Annie to sit beside each other up front had been a colossal mistake. They'd fought about which streets to take and which turns to make the whole way. Now she knew she had to intervene.

"Hey, you two, stop it. Let's get out and see where the sun is coming from. It comes from the east. We'll figure that out and then it's no big deal if we have to walk, seeing that this dump only has – let's see – 15 rooms." She counted as she talked.

They spilled out of the car, which they'd been pleased to find hadn't been repossessed yet. They all wore sunglasses but shielded their eyes with their hands to look up into the flaming bright Nevada summer sky.

"It's noon," Merry noted. "The sun is straight above us. We don't know which way it came from."

"What in blazes is the name of this place? _in _ity _otel." Ginger read off the battered sign that hung above the "Offi_e" door.

"Looks like it has a problem with consonants," Dolly said. "My guess is Sin City Motel."

"That's not the only problem this place has." Merry scrunched up her face as she scanned the building.

"Sure is hard to believe that Balls would live here." Annie fanned her hand in front of her nose to fend off the fusty smell that hung in the air. She went over to the office and peeked in the window, then tried the door even though a sign said "Clo_ed." The door was locked.

She came back to the others and the four of them stood hopelessly in the middle of the cracked and weedy parking lot, scanning the place for any sign of Ballard Benedict. Three cars and two trucks indicated that some of the rooms currently held occupants, although by the looks of the vehicles nobody here was ever going to get too far away.

"I don't see Balls' Porsche. Of course, that would be long gone by now if he lives in a place like this," Dolly observed.

"I don't believe it," Annie clipped. "Balls would never let himself end up like this. He might cheat everybody else, but he'd never cheat himself out of living the high life. I think whatever old man lives here isn't him."

Dolly had to agree. Balls in a claptrap like this? Riding around in one of these jalopies? She couldn't fathom such a thing.

Just then an old man hustled out of the room on the far end. If that was the old guy they'd been told about, they now knew which direction was east. He had a suitcase in hand.

Hesitantly, unsure of themselves, the women inched that way.

Dolly put out her arms like a safety patrol girl, holding back her charges. In a whisper, she said, "Wait. That's a really old guy. I don't think that's Balls."

Ginger agreed. "Yeah, he's too old, too shabby, and too poor."

They watched as the old codger put a key into the door of a fifteen-year-old Ford Pinto. As he opened the door and started to get in, he noticed the mob of women standing in the middle of the parking lot. He paused. Staring at them inquisitively, it appeared as if sudden recognition struck.

"Oh shit!" they heard him cuss. He threw in his suitcase, jumped in, revved it up, squealed in reverse, and jerked forward before they could close the distance between them, leaving them in a cloud of exhaust smoke. The Pinto streaked out of the lot and almost hit a truck in the process, causing an angry blast of a horn.

The women coughed as they hustled away from the flume of fumes and rushed back to their car.

"Keys, Annie. Where are the keys?" Ginger demanded as they piled into the Bentley.

"I don't know." Frantically, Annie scoured through her Gucci bag.

"If you didn't carry a stupid purse as big as a bomber, with more crap in it than a junkyard, you might be able to find them," Ginger scolded.

"Hurry," Dolly pled.

Annie couldn't come up with the keys to save her soul.

"It's too late. He's long gone," Merry sighed.

They all stopped and stared at the street in defeat. The Pinto had vanished.

"Oh, I remember. I put them in my pocket." Annie produced the keys.

"Fat lot of good that does us now," Ginger groused.

"Hey, look." Merry hopped out of the car. "The sign in the window of the office just flipped over. It's open. Well, actually it's 'ope_'."

Somehow having come to feel they must always move in tandem like a gaggle of geese, all four of them crowded into the tiny office. A teenaged boy stared at them with wide dark eyes.

"You want room?" he asked in an accent Dolly couldn't place. "Two rooms? Four?" He held up four fingers, hope registering on his face. His disappointment showed when they didn't want to register.

"No, I'm afraid not. We want to know about the man who stays in the last room." Dolly pointed out the window.

"Man? What man?"

"Um, the old man in the very last room." Dolly pointed more vigorously and silently chastised herself for talking louder, as if that would help overcome a language barrier.

"Oh, him no pay long time. Him gone."

"Could you please tell us his name?"

The teen shrugged. What did he care? He opened a register book, turned it toward them, and pointed to a name. "Him. There."

"Adolf Hitler?"

The others expressed their disbelief and crowded in to look. Sure enough. There it was: "Adolf Hitler."

"Weren't you suspicious of that name?" Ginger asked. But she thought better of it and said, "Oh, sorry. I guess you didn't know."

"Hey," Merry said, "it looks like fake names are the way to go around here. George Washington, Rob Lowe, John Smith, Jim

Bakker, Peter Rabbit." She ran her finger down the page as she read.

"What do you know about the old man?" Dolly asked the teen.

"He gone now."

"I know. But did he ever have visitors? Like women visitors? Do you know anything else about him?"

The boy shrugged.

"Okay. Thank you." Dolly extended her hand to shake, but he bowed instead. "Oh. Okay." She reeled in her hand and gave a stiff bow in return.

Back in the car, Merry offered a suggestion. "I'm hungry. Let's go to the diner."

"We should go back. I mean, we did leave Layla and Malika there without much ado." Dolly wanted to get back to see Layla, but her stomach growled as she spoke.

"I'm sure James is using the time to squeeze out every bit of information he can from Layla. He's good at that," Ginger said. "And he knows how to call room service for lunch."

"Yeah." Annie chuckled. "I bet Winky and Dinky are still there, too, drooling over Malika. That girl doesn't need us there."

Annie pointed the car toward the diner.

Once inside, happy to find their favorite booth available amid the lunchtime rush, they greeted Betty and ordered. "You Don't Have to Say You Love Me" played on the jukebox and Dolly found herself humming along. She loved the '50s music that always played here.

"So," she said once Betty brought their drinks, "was that old man Balls or not?"

"Only if he's really on the outs." Ginger shook her head. "It would've taken a really big fall to make that old guy out of him. The last time I saw him was three years ago. Even though we live in the same city, I'd started avoiding going to his office because he'd become so flashy. Obviously an older man trying to be cool and pretending to be younger. It became painful to watch. We didn't have any business together anymore anyway, except the retirement fund. And I got annual reports in the mail on that. I'm qualified to start drawing from it soon. If it still fucking exists."

The others commented on their faithful annual reports, too. Everyone had received their last one six months earlier.

"Here you go, girls." Betty brought their food, they thanked her, and she hustled away, having no time to chat with the place packed to the gills.

"If that guy wasn't Balls," Merry said, pausing to take a sip of her water, "why did he run away from us."

"If he hasn't paid his rent, he probably owes money to other people, too. He might've thought we were bill collectors." Annie shoved greens around in her salad bowl.

Ginger took a big bite out of her burger and used her napkin to wipe juice dribbled down her chin. She swallowed hard, took a sip of her drink, and wiped her mouth. "You know, I honestly thought Balls would never do anything like this. I know he's self-centered; I know he loves the high life; and I know he was having a hard time adjusting to aging. But think about it: we were his girls. His first girls. He made us and we made him. We all grew up in the business together."

"True," Dolly agreed. "I always felt like we were all in this together. Like a family. Even though not everyone in the family gets along."

"Yeah, that's what I thought, too." Ginger sighed. "I've never told you this and you two are my best friends." Her nods excluded Annie. "So that tells you it was, in a way, sacred to me. You see, not long after we met, early in our careers, Balls and I had a fling. Oh, I thought I was in love. I fantasized that he was, too. When he moved on to somebody else, I was crushed. I never knew who it was. With our crazy schedules and all of us traveling around all the time, and all living in different places, I could never get a fix on it.

Still, he was always kind to me, making sure I had good gigs and stuff. I thought he sorta felt bad about hurting me and would always take care of me in any other way he could. So this betrayal really hurts."

"Huh. I never thought he'd take care of any of us," Annie retorted. "He's always been a son-of-a-bitch player and I was smart enough to know it. Hell, he screwed everybody. He and I had a go of it not long after he dumped you."

"What? You?" Ginger's voice rose to such a shrill that nearby diners turned their heads to gawk.

"Ginger, calm down, honey," Merry soothed. "I dated him for a while having no idea you were, too."

"What?" Ginger screamed. "Did everybody on the planet screw Balls?"

The diner instantly became silent. Not so much as the clink of a fork could be heard. Everyone stared.

Dolly turned to address their audience. "Not me," she proclaimed in a loud, clear voice. "Just for the record, I did not screw Balls."

Titters filtered throughout the crowd. One guy lifted his glass in salute to Dolly. These folks might not know what this was all about, but its salaciousness entertained them. A few shook their heads in dismay, but not many. After all, this was Sin City.

Betty appeared. "Okay, girls, it's time to tone it down. Do it fer me, okay?"

"Okay. Sorry." Ginger shoved her plate away, crossed her arms over her chest, and pouted.

Betty nodded approval. "Listen, is on me as soon as y'all finish. That'll help y'all feel better." She left and silence hung over their table like a threatening thunderhead.

With no more entertainment forthcoming, the other diners lost interest and went back to chowing down.

Dolly ate, knowing that Ginger would have more to say before this was over. She knew her friend. This would not cease so easily. It didn't take long for the storm to hit.

"You," Ginger said, pointing at Merry. "I have no trouble believing Balls took advantage of you and seduced you. You were so naïve when you started." Then she jabbed a finger at Annie, "And now that I think of it, I have no trouble believing you slept with Balls, because you slept with everybody."

"I did not," Annie protested. "I was very selective."

"Oh, sure. That's why your pimp worked the crowds during your performances."

"So what? He only picked the cream of the crop, the guys who were clean and respectable and rich."

"You sold your body for sex."

"Yes, I did, because I wasn't stupid enough to give it away for free like you nitwits."

Dolly decided it was time to end this before it started another knock-down drag-out brawl like they'd had in Ginger's apartment. Besides, Ginger's blood pressure didn't need this.

"Okay. Ginger. Annie. Stop right now. We get it. Balls screwed everybody – except me, although he did try to hit on me once – so now we know he was more devious than we ever imagined. It's done. Put it aside. We have more important things to think about right now, like finding him to see if we can retrieve our money. To that end, we need to gracefully finish our meal, gratefully eat our pie, and get back to the hotel to work with James. We need to get paid for the book, hire a P.I., and let the pro find our tormenter. Now eat. Silently."

She felt like telling each of them to go stand in a corner facing the wall for twenty minutes, her mother's go-to punishment for misbehavior. She'd stood in the corner many a time as a kid.

Ginger slowly pulled back her plate and bit into her burger. Annie nibbled at her salad. Merry gulped down her last bite and Dolly was almost done. The diner started to empty out as people got back to work or gambling, so Betty sat down for a minute when she brought them blueberry pie.

"That Balls was quite the fucker, wasn't he? Literally," Betty said.

Dolly couldn't help but chuckle. "Yeah, he was. Balls Been-a-Dick, like we always say."

Merry said, "His nickname suits him well, that's for sure."

Ginger and Annie avoided each other and the conversation, focusing instead on consuming their pie. Dolly thought they looked like two scared little kids, afraid of what their mean mother might do next. Apparently, she'd knocked some sense into them – if that was possible.

CHAPTER 9

They could hear the laughter even before the elevator doors opened. There they were – Layla and James – sitting in the hot tub on the balcony, sipping on bottles of Coke and laughing about some intimately shared story. Dolly couldn't believe the stab of jealousy she felt at the sight. She loved Layla and was happy she was here. But did the woman really need to get all cozy with James? Well, apparently, yes. The fact that she was a few years younger than Dolly and still had a fabulous figure and ... Dolly stopped herself. She was seventy years old and should be far beyond such petty, junior-high thinking.

But she wasn't.

"Hi, ladies! Come on out here and tell us how it went." James hollered even though they'd left the sliding glass door open, so his voice carried loud and clear.

The four of them went out to the balcony and stepped all over each other's words as they shared the telling of their useless adventure. They apologized for skipping lunch in the penthouse but did come bearing a gift.

Merry produced a covered pie dish. "We've become friends

with a waitress at the '50s Diner. Her name is Betty. She makes the pies for the place, and they're delicious. She sent this for you." She pulled the aluminum foil back to reveal half a blueberry pie.

"Oh, I love blueberries." Layla's face lit up at the sight.

"Great. Even though I'm stuffed from our lunch, I'm in for a piece of pie right now." James hauled himself out of the water and Dolly's breath caught at the sight of him in nothing but swim trunks. He was old, yes, but in great shape. She tried to squelch tacking on "for his age." She hated it when people said that to her. But traitor that she was, the thought pushed its way to the front of her mind. He was perhaps a bit too thin but appealing all the same. His Navy tattoo was now fully visible, the only one he seemed to harbor.

Layla got out, too, and while she and James toweled off, Dolly and Merry went to the kitchen to dole out the pie.

"I'm gonna grab my suit and get in the tub," Ginger announced as she trotted to her room.

"Me, too," Annie said as she did the same.

Watching them go, Merry said, "Do you think those two have any idea how much alike they are sometimes?"

"Nope. No idea. And if we told them, they'd deny it to their graves."

While they dished up succulent slices of pie, Layla went to her room to change but James, seeing that he'd have to go down the elevator to get to his room, threw a towel over his shoulders, draped another towel over a kitchen counter stool, and sat down to eat. Dolly adored his appreciation of food.

"Where's Malika?" Dolly asked as she handed over the plate with an extra large slice.

Merry retrieved a fork from a drawer and slid it over to accompany the plate. Then she leaned in with her elbows on the counter while Dolly went around the counter and sat next to James.

"She went to the convention with the boys." He dug in and consumed a huge bite. "Um, this is delicious. Thanks so much." He swallowed another big bite. At this rate, Dolly thought he'd be done in three more bites.

She hesitated. She didn't want to sound like she was prying – although she was – but she wanted to know what James and Layla had been talking about. Merry saved her.

"Did Layla give you some good stories for the book?" Merry asked.

"Oh, yes. Great stuff." He'd politely swallowed before answering, which pleased Dolly. He didn't talk with his mouth full. "I'm sure she's told you this, but the history of belly dancing is fascinating. I have to include it in the book, starting with fertility dancing in ancient times. Then, when a woman was in labor, men would sit outside the hut and beat drums to provide rhythm to help her breathe. That's so cool. Later, women in harems not only vied for the sheik's attention but entertained each other and their eunuchs. Then it became a rather risqué but popular source of entertainment at nighttime gathering places." He raised his eyebrows to hint at the underground nature of the dance. "And Little Egypt was one of the first to bring it to the states when she danced at the Chicago World's Fair in 1893."

Dolly nodded, having heard the story years ago from Layla. "And then Theda Bara brought it to silent film."

"And she was considered to be so wicked," Merry added, and they all chuckled.

"You would have loved seeing Layla dance." Dolly felt commendable for saying so and privately patted herself on the back for her largesse. "She was amazing."

"Yeah," Merry agreed as she straightened up, held her arms out to her sides, and swayed her hips. "She did a historical timeline of the art, starting in a sort of primitive robe that covered her whole costume. Then that came off and she had on her harem costume, but all wrapped in veils."

Dolly picked up the story. "The veils came off, one by one, until she had on a top like a bathing suit top covered in gold coins, a wide belt that matched the top, and her flowy long skirt. Her costumes were gorgeous, and she made them all herself."

Merry spun around to illustrate twirling a skirt as best she could in street clothes and came back to lean on the counter again. "She did floorwork like you wouldn't believe. Backbends to die for."

"Yes, and that's probably why I'm on a cane now." Layla tittered good-naturedly as she came up behind them, leaning on her spiffy walking stick. "I did those backbends one too many times and ruined my knees. At least, that gives me something to blame besides old age." She sat down at the counter on the other side of James, and Merry served her pie.

Ginger and Annie emerged from their rooms in tandem, Ginger with a robe over her swimsuit and Annie with no robe over her suit. Exposing her body, at any age, was fine with Annie.

Ginger said, "I was thinking we could all work from the hot tub for a while."

"Why don't you two go ahead and enjoy yourselves?" James suggested. "I want to talk to Dolly and Merry for a bit about the history of burlesque."

Ginger and Annie started to trot off, but Layla stopped them. "Wait." The two women turned back. "I have something to tell all of you and haven't had a chance yet." Layla stuck out her left hand, where a diamond ring sparkled on her ring finger. "I'm engaged and getting married next month."

Dolly couldn't believe she hadn't noticed the ring, it was such a stunner. Her emotions collided with each other inside her mind. Yes, she was happy for her beloved friend. But she was even more relieved that Layla wasn't interested in James.

"That's wonderful!" Dolly slid off her stool and went around James to grab Layla in a hug. "I'm so happy for you."

Ginger and Merry went to Layla, too, offering hugs and well wishes. But Annie had a question first. "Is he rich? It isn't worth getting married unless he is. Too many men our age want a nurse or a purse. You've got to be careful."

Layla laughed. "Oh, Annie. You would think of that. Not that it's any of your business, but he isn't rich and he isn't poor. He's a retired engineer with a nice retirement. We won't need to worry. In fact, he wanted to help me get my money from Balls, but I wanted to do it. I don't want him to feel like I can't take care of myself. And I don't want to feel that way, either."

"That's good, Layla. Continue to be your own woman." Dolly nodded approval.

"Well," Annie sighed, "that's nice, I guess, but it's easier to be your own woman if he's rich." With that she turned on her bare heels and strutted to the hot tub. Ginger scuttled along in her wake.

Layla watched them go. "Do you think we'll ever know what really went on with Annie and that marriage she had?"

Dolly stared at Annie as she stretched out one long leg after another to slip into the hot tub. "Nah. Probably not."

James glanced toward the balcony. "Maybe it's better that way."

They moved to the sofa and Dolly began her story about the history of burlesque.

"Burlesque is as old as anybody knows. A precursor to what we know today was popular in Elizabethan times with performances that mocked politicians, Shakespeare, and even royalty. Eventually, women in tights – which was very risqué – performed, too. By the time it made its way over here, it was a variety show that included everything like when we first started in the business." Dolly waved a hand to indicate that "we" included all of them as dancers.

"What's the difference between burlesque and vaudeville?" James asked. "I've always wondered about that."

"Burlesque was always considered to be the bawdier of the two and by the time it reached the states it always included scantily clothed women," Dolly explained. "Vaudeville was originally cleaner, with a wider variety of acts. They had music, singers, skits, comedians, kid and animal acts, slapstick comedy, jugglers, acrobats, dancers, and some off-color jokes, but not as off-color as burlesque. Burlesque had the music and singers and comedians, too, but the highlight was always the sexy dancer at the end. Although, some vaudeville shows became pretty bawdy, too. At times, I suppose burlesque and vaudeville were one and the same. Vaudeville was popular from around 1880 to the early 1930s. I read a book about it once. It's fascinating."

"Yeah, too bad it died," Merry said. "I suspect if it hadn't been for nearly naked women burlesque would have died sooner, too. But burlesque shows were enormously popular, especially before movies and even up until the time before TV."

"That's when the burlesque greats performed," Layla added. "Gypsy Rose Lee, Ann Curio, Blaze Starr, Candy Barr, Sally Rand. By the time we came along in the '40s and '50s, burlesque was still doing well."

"Yeah," Merry chimed in, "but by the '60s strip clubs had become more prolific, with pole dancers and a lot more nudity than we ever displayed. And pornographic movies became more public, with adult theaters popping up everywhere."

"Like Champs." James didn't miss the irony. "What we do helped kill your live shows."

"Yes, that's true." Dolly had to agree.

"Burlesque died for a while," Layla explained, "but now it's being picked up by drag queens. I've seen a couple of their shows here in Vegas and they're really fun. Although, some of the performers are good and others are not. But it's a great atmosphere, no matter what. I checked in case we wanted to go see one, but none are playing right now."

"I always think of Christine Jorgensen when I hear about those shows," Dolly added. "Do you remember Christine?" she asked James.

"Sure, the first man to have surgery and become a woman, at least the first that the public heard about here in the states. A transgender woman, they call it. When was that? 1950?"

"Early 1950s," Dolly said. "She had the surgeries in Denmark because nobody here would do it. We knew her after she became an entertainer."

"Her act was fab-u-lous," Ginger added. "That girl could sing. And she was so funny! Audiences loved her. Her favorite song was 'I Enjoy Being a Girl.' So perfect."

Dolly started to sing, arms spread wide. Merry joined in, ending with a rousing "I enjoy being a girl!"

James and Layla clapped, and soggy applause could be heard from the balcony.

"Her performance was incredible," Dolly said. "And her rapport with the audience was great. No matter how many people were there, she made you feel like she was performing just for you."

"Yeah," Merry said, "in our world of entertainment it was hard to understand why anyone would not absolutely love her. It was heartbreaking that so many people out there in the world made fun of her and rejected her."

"That brings up a question for you, Dolly, about prejudice," James said. "You're the only African American in the group. Most dancers were white, but the bands and singers were mostly black."

"Yes, that's right."

"Did you and the other black entertainers run into any problems with racists?"

"Oh my, yes. In fact, Christine and I used to compare notes about mistreatment because of who we were, me because of my dark skin and her because of her sexual orientation. We admitted that as performers we had it easier than many. When people go to see a performer, that's what they want. Professionally, we were a bit insulated, at least on stage. But still there were plenty of horror stories to go around. On the other hand, we were sometimes surprised by who cropped up to support us, people we never would have suspected. I remember the first time that happened for me.

TOLEDO, Ohio, 1950

DOLLY O'DARE, Aretha Franklin, Cab Calloway, and the band got off the bus in a drizzle of rain. Umbrellas popped up amongst them, but not everyone managed to get covered while waiting to pull their luggage out of the bin on the side of the vehicle. Many a coat or suit lapel was pulled up to fend off the damp chill. A flashing neon sign above announcing the Pink Parrott blurred in the foggy mist.

Suitcases and instrument cases in hand, heads ducked against the wet and cold, the first in line hurried toward the front door of the club.

"You can't come in here." A bruiser of a man stood out front, arms akimbo, barring their way. A white man, he made no secret of his distaste for this group of black people.

Still, Cab tried to be conciliatory. "Oh, we know you aren't open yet, but we're the entertainment. We need to get in to set up before the doors open."

He tried to skirt around the man, but the brute stuck out an arm with biceps the size of a tree trunk.

"I know who you are. You can't come in because niggers have to use the back door."

Dolly vacillated between shuddering in fear and being pissed off. Things like this had rarely happened during her short career. She and Aretha looked at each other with wide eyes and impulsively stood closer together in solidarity under their shared umbrella.

A grumble rose up from the band, but Cab motioned for them to quiet down. "Follow me," he said to them as he turned to head for the back. They all knew it would do no good to argue. None of them could afford to lose a week's pay.

They'd only taken a few steps when a sleek, black sedan pulled up. A man who looked like somebody had tried to stuff a bulldozer into an expensive suit got out, opened an umbrella, and opened the back door. An elderly white man in a classy suit got out of the back, a real gentleman type, Dolly thought. He took the umbrella and stood there for a moment, surveying the group. Another man, much like the first, got out of the car. The two big guys appeared to be bodyguards to the older man. Now terror rose in Dolly's throat, and she could only imagine that the same was true for the others.

"Oh, oh," Aretha whispered, "If those men decide to cause more trouble, this isn't going to be pretty."

"What's going on here?" the older man asked.

"Mr. Levi, sir, these nig …," the bouncer said, but interrupted himself when he saw the look on the man's face. "Um, those people want to go in the front door." His voice had deteriorated into a whine.

"And?" the man queried.

"And, well, I told them to go around back, of course."

"Of course?" the gentleman said. "Why?"

"Well, sir," the bouncer replied, nervously clearing his throat, "you can see why."

The man nodded to the men Dolly now thought of as his henchman, who went over to stand on either side of the bouncer.

"Apologize," the man said.

"What?"

"You heard me."

"But …"

The henchman each took one of his arms and carried him to the street, where they deposited him with such force he fell into a puddle.

"Don't ever let me see you near my club again."

The now former bouncer stumbled until he managed to stand up and run away.

Dolly was stunned. Apparently, this older guy was a force to be reckoned with.

He immediately turned his attention to the damp ensemble in front of him. "Please, please. Come in." He held the door open himself until everyone had entered.

Inviting them to take off their wet jackets, he went behind the bar and offered to pour drinks to help everyone "warm up." Then he held up his glass of bourbon, indicating that he had something to say.

"I want to welcome you to my club. I'm Sal Levi, the owner. I'm sorry for what happened out there. He was new and didn't know how we operate. Unfortunately, there are far too many ignorant people like that in this world. I know I've never had it as hard as you, but being a Jew gives me a bit of a feeling for what it's like. I've been shut out of many places. Churches. Businesses. An occasional restaurant. The golf club I wanted to join. Hell, I had to buy the damned place to get in. Then I invited all my Jewish friends to join to piss off the other members." That drew a chorus of snickers. "Anyway, we'll see to it that kind of thing doesn't happen to you again." He nodded at his henchman, who stood at attention at opposite ends of the room. Dolly noticed that half a dozen other men like them had appeared. She elbowed Aretha, who saw them, too. "Here's to a prosperous and enjoyable week." Mr. Levi lifted his glass in salute and everyone reciprocated.

"Thank you, Mr. Levi," Cab said. "We look forward to having a great week."

As the band started to set up, Dolly and Aretha pulled Cab aside.

"Who is that Mr. Levi?" Dolly asked.

"Yeah," Aretha added, "That guy out front seemed awfully scared of him."

"Children, haven't you ever heard of Sal Levi?"

They shook their heads.

"He's one of the biggest, baddest mob bosses in this part of the country. His Jewish gang started out pretty much as thugs, but over the years he's become a legitimate businessman who owns half this city. But everybody knows he's still got plenty of illegitimate businesses going on, too. Thank God we're on his good side." Amused, Cab went back to helping the band set up.

"Miss O'Dare."

She turned to see one of the henchmen addressing her. She figured she'd need to learn his name before long.

"Yes?"

"Mr. Levi would like to speak to you. Please follow me."

After what Cab had told her, she was overcome with trepidation but knew she dare not refuse. She looked at Aretha for help, but her friend had no choice but to shrug, so Dolly followed the man to an opulent office in the back of the club.

"Miss O'Dare," Mr. Levi said, "please have a seat." He'd been sitting behind his desk but gallantly stood when she entered the room. He pointed to a chair across the desk from him.

"I, um, well, I need to get into my costume in a minute."

"That can wait." He sat back down.

Dolly did as instructed and sat.

"I would have saved this for later, but I have to leave town in an hour on business. I saw you dance recently when I was in Detroit."

"Yeah? Huh."

"Yes, and I was very impressed. You're fantastic. A beautiful young woman."

"Oh, Mr. Levi, I don't …"

He held up a hand to stop her. "Oh no. I'm not propositioning you. Good heavens, I have a wife and five daughters. The last thing I need is another woman in my life. No, no, what I want is a business arrangement. I'd like to book you for a week every two months for the next year. I'd book this whole crew but Cab and his band are already booked out for the year, and I hear Aretha has a record deal. She's headed to be a star." He leaned in with his forearms on his desk. "And so are you."

All she could manage to say was, "Oh. Thanks. Okay."

He clapped the desk with the palm of his hand. "Good. It's a deal." He stuck out his hand and she shook it having no idea exactly what she'd done.

LAS VEGAS, 1995

"IT TURNED out what I'd done was give my career a rocket boost. Mr. Levi hooked me up with Balls, who made it all happen after that. I have to admit that, as much as it pains me to do so. I worked at that club for a year, and then Mr. Levi was arrested for solicitation of murder, conspiracy to commit murder, collusion, racketeering, tax evasion, fraud, and a bunch of other charges. He was sent to prison and his businesses were closed down. The rumor was the Sicilian mafia had set him up so they could take over the turf and there was a gang war where lots of guys got killed. Obviously, the Jewish gang lost the battle.

"I visited Mr. Levi every time I worked in Toledo. It was hard for me to imagine he'd done all those things, although I know he did. To me, he was a gentleman with a big heart, a father figure who loved his wife and children, and who was kind to me. He died ten years later, still in prison."

Merry shook her head. "A father figure in prison. You sure do know how to pick them, Dolly."

Dolly couldn't resist a teasing retort. "Hey, at least I didn't fall in love with a priest in a cemetery."

Merry laughed. "Touché."

CHAPTER 10

James switched gears. "Those days when burlesque was still good, in the '40s and '50s," what was your favorite part of performing?"

"Connecting with the audience," Layla immediately replied.

"Yes, that was it," Merry agreed.

"Uh huh," Dolly added. "Making people happy."

Ginger, wrapped in her robe, came up and caught the question. "I agree. I loved having fun with the people who came to our shows."

Layla motioned to Ginger to sit beside her, and Ginger obliged. "I loved your routines, Ginger. That cowgirl thing you did was so much fun. James, you should have seen her in her cowgirl hat, leather chaps with not much underneath, a whip, and a cap gun. And a cowgirl vest with nothing under it, either, except her pasties."

"And the way you could do that twirling thing we talked about." Dolly snickered.

"What twirling thing?" James wanted to know.

"Our pasties," Merry revealed. "Ginger taught us how to twirl them in opposite directions. She was a master at it. Crowds loved that."

"Wait. Nobody ever taught me how to do that." Annie appeared, toweling off but still managing to drip on the floor. "Show me."

"No. My goodness. We're too old for that," Ginger scoffed.

"Listen, I didn't do that, either." Layla tried to mollify Annie. "I didn't strip down that far. I always had a top on."

"I liked all of our routines." Ginger veered away from pasties. "Merry, your first one, when you tore off your nun's habit, was good, but when you started that second one, where you played not a religious sister but the goodie-two-shoes homebody." She chuckled. "That was genius."

"The cupcakes were genius." Dolly smacked her lips.

"I admit," Merry said, turning to James to explain, "that did work well. When I first started dancing, I was still mad at the world. But Dolly suggested that I tone it down. Instead of ripping off my nun's habit like I was mad at the church and men and everyone else on earth, which I was, she said it would be better to make it look like I was a woman coming into her own."

"I wanted you to make it something positive rather than negative," Dolly explained.

"Yes, and it worked. That eventually evolved into me doing different routines where a woman breaks out of all kinds of traditional roles. A secretary, a teacher, things like that. But when I hit on being a merry homemaker, like men imagined the girl next door, who passed out cupcakes that I really did make myself, it was like I'd hit gold." She shook her head in wonder. "I started out wearing a frilly bib apron, with a big bow holding up my hair." She waved her hands down her torso to illustrate what a bib apron covered. "I'd pretend to make the cupcakes there on stage while dancing around. Then I'd go into the audience to dance while giving out the cupcakes to the people in the front. Then the waitresses would come in and make sure everybody else got one, too.

I'd go back to the stage and, now done with my domestic chores, let down my hair and take off my apron to reveal my body. It was so simple yet so popular."

"I remember," Ginger said, "that one old guy who came in every night when we were working the same club one time."

"Yeah, he said his wife had died and nobody made him home-made cupcakes anymore."

"And you, being you …" Ginger reached over and patted Merry's arm "… made him extras to take home once you found out he was widowed."

"That sounds like a great routine. I can see why audiences loved the cupcake stripper." James had been taking notes and paused. "So, how about you two? What were your routines like?" He pointed his pen at Annie and Dolly, satisfied with the descriptions of Layla's, Ginger's, and Merry's performance routines.

"Oh, mine was easy. I used big fans. Men went wild." Annie hadn't bothered to go change out of her swimsuit and had plopped her soggy derrière down on the couch. "Didn't they?" She looked at the other women for validation.

"Yes. I must admit," Dolly said, "they did."

"It was easy. I just copied Sally Rand. She was a famous fan dancer earlier on. I saw her dance once and said to myself, 'I could do that.' So I did."

James nodded as he took notes. Then he turned to Dolly. "And what were your performances like?"

Dolly considered the question. She could give a quick, shallow answer. Or she could tell the truth.

MIAMI, Florida, 1951

. . .

THE BLUES MUSIC infused her soul with rhythm, taking command of her body. Her being belonged to the beat; her mind drifted away with the cadence of the drum; her legs moved of their own accord, following the legacy of the dance.

Dolly was performing the final number of her set, a sultry strut across the stage, this time lost in her own world and not looking at her audience. They were already hooked, anyway. Over the past couple of years, she'd improved her show to the point it had become famous in the world of burlesque. The name Dolly O'Dare had become synonymous with not only sexiness, but fun, as well.

She started her set with a frolicking Danzón, the traditional Cuban dance she learned on previous visits to Miami. She wore a colorful gown, tailormade to her specifications and encrusted with sequins. She reveled in grabbing the ruffly tiered skirt and flitting it around. Slit all the way up her thigh on one side, the gown afforded plenty of opportunity to showcase her lissome legs. She also carried the customary hand fan, opening and closing it coquettishly.

The dance's African-European roots thrilled her, knowing that she performed a ritual that connected her to others long gone from this earth, kindred souls who had understood her primitive need to move to music. She felt as if she were one with those strangers while she performed their dance, as if they had slipped into her body to savor the bliss of physical movement once again. She danced for all of them as well as for herself.

She'd altered the Danzón slightly, naturally, to fit stage work. Instead of stopping at one point to flirt with a partner, as they did in the original version, she'd stop and hold the fan up to her face to cover her mouth and nose, allowing her to flutter her eyelashes at her audience. Well-rehearsed, the band stopped, too, and silence filled the house for the measured moments she stared down at her patrons, flirting with them as if they were her lovers. Then she'd moved again, perfectly hitting the first note when the band picked up.

The audiences always went berserk over that number. She especially got a kick out of times when some of them were so invigorated by the music and the show, they couldn't sit still. They'd get up and mimic her moves like they had on this night. That proved a perfect segue to her next number where she played with the audience and brought people up on stage to dance with her. She liked picking out the shyest-looking men and women to help nudge them out of their shells. The band always went along and came up with perfect off-the-cuff snips of music.

The bands were usually very good, but this one was fabulous. They were Lawrence Welk players from the popular musical variety TV show that didn't film during the summer, so they did this on the side. Dolly thought that show didn't even begin to highlight their talents. They could play jazz, rhythm-and-blues, Latin, classical, show tunes, rock-and-roll, country-western, sing-along. Name it and they could play it. She felt truly blessed to live in this world of music and movement. And mischief and mayhem, too, when off stage.

But she didn't think of any of the turmoil around the constant travel and tribulations of a gypsy life. Not while she was on stage. The stage made it all worthwhile.

At some point in her show – she liked to play it by ear – the tiered skirt would come off, leaving her in a skin-tight gown. Usually, because the tiered skirt was slit up the side and had a simple hook at the waist, she'd take it off and wrap it like a cape around an audience member she had on stage. Portly men were the most fun. She'd also hand them her fan and encourage them to flirt with it. When that rollicking act finished, she moved on to more intimate fare.

So here she was, doing her final number on her last night of this gig in Miami. After being lost in her own world, the music tugged at her mind to remind her she'd reached the point where she needed to reconnect with her audience. She lowered her chin and looked at the crowd with hooded eyes and winked. Slowly, seductively, she slipped one dress strap off her shoulder. She looked at the crowd again and grinned. They applauded and whooped appreciatively. She hooked a finger under the other strap, threw out a glance, and removed her finger without releasing it. They howled with laughter. She turned so they could see while she reached back and unzipped her dress halfway. She looked over her shoulder with an expression of indecision, shook her head, and pulled the zipper back up. The audience reaction was exactly what she expected – good-humored disappointment. Acting as if their response made her feel bad, she turned back to face them, quickly unzipped the glimmery gown, and let it cascade to the floor. There she stood, her arms thrust up into the air as the band played to a final crescendo, a pair of shiny panties and sparkly pasties her only signs of modesty.

Dolly loved this ending to her show. She didn't always do it, though. Sometimes she didn't strip at all, which only brought them back the next night. But on most nights, she felt like gifting them with what they wanted. This was one of those nights.

She turned around again with her back to them and twitched her butt cheeks, which sent her fans into a frenzy. With that, she flounced off stage. Never forgetting her signature wave, she stuck her arm out from the side curtain as the fracas rose again. She never went back for an encore, having given all that she chose to give. She'd made them happy, and that made her happy. Now her life was her own again, until next time.

CHAPTER 11

$\mathcal{L}$as Vegas, 1995

"Wow. I wish I could've seen all your routines. Amazing stuff. I can just picture them in my head." James looked directly at Dolly. "Okay. So, let's move on to the famous people you've met. Who impressed you? Who didn't? Is there anything about anybody famous that people would be surprised about?"

"How about a break first," Merry suggested.

"Yeah, I need to get out of these damp clothes and get a drink. Can I get one for anybody else?" Ginger got up and went to the kitchen.

Once the whole crew was back on the couch, dry clothes on and wet refreshments at hand, James turned on the recorder again and set it on coffee table. As always, he took notes with pen and paper. It was back to the business at hand. James had warned them that the next day would be his last, and they would need to cover sex and anything else they felt had been missed. He'd be taking the red-eye back to Detroit at midnight tomorrow night.

Dolly had hated hearing that bit of news. She'd only known him for two days and already she would miss him.

"Well, let's see," she said. "Famous people. To start with, we all met amazing musicians and singers."

"Yeah, like B.B. King. He was always a favorite." Ginger sat next to James and tapped on his notepad with the tip of her finger, emphasizing that the iconic bluesman needed to be written down. James obliged. "He sang *The Thrill is Gone*, but the thrill was never gone when he was on stage."

Merry chuckled. "Ah huh. And there was always a lot of mysterious smoke in the air when he played. Everybody sure was happy."

"Hell, he'd light up a joint right on stage and pass it around to everybody, including the audience." Annie comedically imitated smoking a toke. "He was very generous that way."

The others couldn't help but laugh.

"But that didn't impair his playing. Oh my god, that man can play. Even before he was famous, dancing to his guitar was like drifting into another realm of existence." Dolly fluttered her hand to connote floating away.

"And working with Jimmy Durante was loads of fun, too. He and Pookie knew each other," Annie bragged.

"Oh, he was fun," Ginger agreed. "I loved it when he would emcee the show and do his comedy and play the piano and sing. He brought life to the room." She got up and sang a few lines of his famous number *Inka Dinka Doo*, which was greeted with applause and whistles. She bowed and sat down.

"Uh huh, he was one of a kind," Merry added. "He always teased us dancers in such a fun way. It was like advertising us to the audience and building up anticipation for our routines. What an unselfish pro."

"Cab Callaway, too," Dolly noted. "That man could sing and

dance, all while leading his band. He was an amazing performer. Plus he was handsome as all get-out."

Female heads bobbed agreement all around, accompanied by moans of "uh huh."

"As for singers, I think most of us..." Merry looked from woman to woman "...at one time or another worked with Aretha Franklin, Della Reese, The Four Tops, Mel Torme, Vic Damone."

"Louie Armstrong."

"Jackie Wilson."

"Sarah Vaughn."

"Dinah Washington."

"Fats Walker."

They threw names out so fast James had to ask them to repeat one at a time so he could get them down.

"Yeah, especially in the early days before they became famous. They would make the club circuit just like we did."

"So you met lots of performers, many who became famous. What about others? Politicians. Actors and actresses. Business tycoons. Did you become friends with anyone like that or date anyone like that?" James wanted to get to the good stuff.

"Well, I did meet my Pookie while I was dancing. He was one of the richest men in the country. A famous business tycoon, like you say. And, yes, I did have sex with him." She tittered at that. "Lots of it."

"Where were you working when you met him?"

"The Vagabond Room in Cleveland. He was there on business for a few days. He came in every night to see me. That's all it took. He was hooked."

"I bet. What other famous people did any of you meet?" James looked around for answers.

They gave him names of movie stars and politicians who came into the clubs, who would schmooze with them. Annie had dated a few B-movie actors before getting married. Merry ran into Elvis once by accident in a drug store in Memphis. Ginger saw stars all the time in Vegas, so didn't think much of that anymore.

"But Dolly has the best story about meeting famous people," Merry said.

"Yeah, Dolly, come on. Go ahead and tell James," Ginger coaxed. "Start with the famous comedian and then the basketball player and then the dictator."

James' eyebrows arched in interest. "Yes, Dolly, do tell."

She took a sip of her 7-Up to bolster her strength for the telling of this wacky tale. "Well, Wolff Garstonn came into Forbidden City, where I was working." She knew that James, being in the business he was in, would be familiar with the section of San Francisco that had for many years been known for its superb burlesque clubs. Sailors, entertainers, businessmen – they all came to Forbidden City when in the Bay Area. "He was doing a gig at the Orpheum, the famous old Gothic-style theater. He saw my show and came backstage after my number. I was flattered. After all, he was really big time. He'd taken the country by storm with his hilarious routine."

"Hilarious without being raunchy. He portrayed a befuddled, smoking streetcleaner, talking about all the people who walked by," James said. "I remember it well. Laughed my ass off."

"Yes, so you can understand why I was excited. He was famous and rich, and smart, to top it off. He was awfully nice, too. So when he asked me out for dinner the next night – we both had Sunday nights off – I said yes. I was so excited, the next day I spent an hour trying to decide what to wear. Well, little did I realize that Wolff didn't care what I wore. He didn't want me to wear anything at all."

The phone rang and Annie popped up off the couch to answer.

"Ah ha …. Okay …. Great!" She hung up and did a little jig as she came back to stand in front of them. "I have a surprise for everybody. Except you." She pointed at James. "You girls are going to love it! Gotta skedaddle. I'll be back in a jiff."

She grabbed her purse and skedaddled.

"I wonder what in hell she's got going." Ginger shook her head at the elevator doors as they closed.

"I wouldn't even begin to venture a guess," Dolly said.

"Okay, back to Wolff Garstonn." James nodded at Dolly.

"Yes. Wolff. Well ..."

SAN FRANCISCO, 1952

"THAT STEAK DINNER WAS WONDERFUL, Wolff. Thank you." Dolly had thoroughly enjoyed their evening in the Venetian Room at his hotel, the Fairmont.

"How about a nightcap in my room?"

She'd expected the invitation, figuring they'd have sex before the evening was over. After all, she was single, he was single, and they liked each other a lot. "Sure," she said.

What she hadn't expected was what happened next.

They were naked on his bed, making out passionately – or so she thought – when he stopped to open a brown paper bag on the nightstand. He pulled out four pieces of rope and held them up.

"How about this?" he asked.

It caught her off guard, seeming off-kilter. It didn't go with the ambiance he'd set up in his bedroom. Romantic low lights. The scent of fresh roses. A silk bedspread. Soft music.

"O-o-oh," she stammered. "Well, I don't know. I've never done anything like that before." She'd heard plenty of stories from other performers in the dressing rooms of clubs about how some people like "bondage," so she knew what was going on here. She just hadn't expected to be called upon to do it herself.

"Really?" He seemed incredulous. "That's okay. Of course you don't have to if you don't want to. But could you do it to me? I mean, usually two people take turns, but if you do me, then I can do whatever you want for you." His gaze was so hopeful, she couldn't say no. "There are a bunch of toys in there, too. You'll love them." He nobbed his head toward the open package.

She peeked inside the bag and saw a fuzzy pink thing, a short stick with a bulb on the end for reasons she could only imagine, and more paraphernalia underneath those. "Um, all right, but you'll have to tell me what to do."

"Sure. No problem." He did a face-up spread eagle on the bed and instructed her to bind his wrists to the bedpost and his ankles to the footboard. Dolly didn't quite get the thrill in that, but to each his own, she supposed. She'd always been fine with two simple naked bodies. But she did as instructed. Once he was bound, which excited him mightily, he asked if she would "mind" mounting him. When she did, she found that she was surprised at how much fun she was having. It was a kick to be in charge.

"Talk dirty to me. Please," he whimpered.

"You nasty boy … Holy shit! There's somebody else in the room!" Dolly screamed, jumped up, and covered herself with a pillow. She squinted in the dim light. Who in hell was this?

"Oh, hi, girls." Wolff lifted his head as far as bondage would allow. "Dolly, this is Cindy and Mindy."

"MiMi, you bad boy," one of them, the Asian one with gorgeous waist-length straight black hair that Dolly could never dream of having, cooed. She slapped him on his thigh.

He squealed in delight.

"Hi, Dolly," the white woman, apparently named Cindy, if that was indeed her real name, greeted her while shedding her own clothes. This one had poufy blond hair that Dolly also could never hope to have.

MiMi disrobed, as well.

"I hope you don't mind," Wolff said to Dolly. "I like three at a time."

"Come on, honey," MiMi insisted, pulling at Dolly's protective pillow. "You've got a great body. Let's enjoy it."

Dolly was dumbfounded. The women proved to be voracious lovers and as uninhibited as two bitch dogs in heat. Cindy clasped Dolly's hand to try to get her onto the bed when they went to work on Wolff, who now sounded like a genuine howling wolf, but soon forgot the outlier who stood at the side of the bed. Dolly watched in fascination as the two women not only plied their trade on the man, but also lusted after each another. MiMi dug into the brown paper bag, came up with the pink toy, and knew how to use it. Its buzzing whirled and faded in a repetitive cadence. Dolly couldn't see exactly what MiMi was doing with it but, whatever it was, it drove Wolff wild.

Nobody noticed when Dolly quietly picked up her clothes, dressed, and tip-toed out of the room. Softly closing the door behind her, she paused. A giggle escaped unexpectedly. "Yup," she whispered. "To each his own. And that is not my own."

Las Vegas, 1995

James chuckled. "His act was so goody-two-shoes. Of course, you never know what someone's real life is like when they're acting."

"Yeah," Dolly said, "I never would have guessed that. But he was very sweet about it later. He sent me flowers, a note, and a mink coat. I gave the coat to my church's charity for the homeless, so they could sell it. Wolff said he'd assumed I'd be into that kind of thing because I was an exotic dancer. He apologized for what he called his 'stupidity.' But it turned out he wasn't the real problem. A much bigger problem developed that was related to that."

The phone rang and Merry got up to answer. After a genial conversation, she came back to the couch and announced that Malika had called to say the boys at the imposter convention at the Flamingo had spread the word about Balls Benedict, and there were a number of people who knew him and thought they'd seen him hanging around. The whole place was out to find the thief who'd robbed retired dancers.

"That's great," Ginger said. "We have help finding the scumbag."

"And," Merry added, "Malika's been invited to perform on stage tomorrow night at eight o'clock. She wants us all to come."

Layla clapped with delight. "Oh, she's so good! I want you all to see her."

It was agreed that everyone would go, even James, who would need to leave for the airport afterward.

"Did she say when she'd be coming back over here?" Layla asked of her granddaughter.

"Ah, no. I didn't think of that."

"Okay. Just wondering. I also wonder if she's in love with one of those boys yet and which one it might be, Superman or Elvis."

An impromptu survey in the room revealed that the odds were even up for either man. James refused to vote.

The elevator chimed and Annie returned just in time to cast her vote for Elvis. She carried a large Dior bag and announced that she had a surprise for all them, something they could enjoy after James left for the evening.

James fidgeted with his pen, wanting to get back to Dolly's teaser of a story about bigger problems after her debacle with the comedian. But Annie chattered on about how much fun they would have later on.

When the girls all got up to take a break, James put down his notepad and pen and got up. Walking out onto the balcony, he stretched his arms out along the railing and took in the sights. It was late afternoon, but that didn't really matter in Las Vegas.

Colorful neon lit the day as far as the eye could see. Dolly came up beside him.

"How do you think it's going?" she asked.

He turned toward her. "The stories so far are great. I won't have any trouble folding them into a marketable book. But I must say, I've worked with lots of women before on movies, adjusting scripts during filming. It's never been like this. This is a bit like trying to catch tadpoles. They slip right out of your hands."

"Did you catch tadpoles in the creek when you were growing up?"

"Of course. Didn't every kid?"

"No."

They laughed. Dolly adored his laughter. And his patience, talent, attitude, the lines etched into his cheeks. Okay, she told herself to stop.

But James didn't stop. "Dolly, how about when we're both back in Detroit, I take you out to dinner. You up for that?"

"Sure." She wondered if she sounded too eager, like a teenager. She also wondered what her darling dead Otis would think. She hadn't given another man an iota of thought until James came along.

"Good. It's a date. Now, how about we get back to it." He motioned toward the living room. "I want to hear your next story."

<h1 style="text-align:center">CHAPTER 12</h1>

"I met Rooster Farmer at a club in Chicago. I'd dated Wolff, so when I met this guy, I wondered why men take on animal names. Rooster's real name was Robert Farmer, but he told me he'd had that chicken nickname since he'd been a kid. We hit it off right away. He was six feet six inches tall and was a basketball player for the Harlem Globetrotters."

"I remember him." James sounded enthusiastic that this story promised to provide a sports scoop. "He was a great player. Very talented."

"Yes. And a perfect gentleman. At first."

James stopped writing and looked at Dolly. "He wasn't always a gentleman?"

"Oh just wait. You'll see what I mean. One night, I was at their game and the announcer hadn't shown up. He had a tendency to get snockered senseless. So I offered to announce the game. I've always been a huge sports fan, and I wasn't shy, that's for sure. I ended up having a blast and the crowd loved it. Of course, I couldn't take on that job full-time because I had my own schedule to keep, but they'd been invited to Cuba to play and asked me to

113

come along. I would work with the announcer, if he stayed sober enough to do it at all, and I'd provide some 'color,' some funny bits. So I cleared my schedule for the trip. By then Rooster and I'd been dating for about three weeks. I was crazy about him, and I believed he felt the same for me."

Dolly took a sip of her soda pop and looked around the group. She had everyone's attention. Painful memories flooded back as she described what happened next.

CUBA, 1953

"GREETINGS. Welcome to Cuba. My name is Fidel Castro. I am a basketball fan and am pleased to have you here in my country. I was on the committee that invited you here."

The man's speech sounded rehearsed, and Dolly guessed that English didn't come naturally to him. But he was easy to understand, and he certainly was good-looking. Tall, with a scruffy short beard, he was very appealing, especially in military fatigues. But, of course, none of that mattered, because the love of her life stood right beside her.

This Señor Castro extended his hand to her first, she assumed because she was the only woman in the group, and she reciprocated. But instead of shaking, he placed his other hand on top of hers and stared into her eyes. Ah, she thought, a typical gesture of male domination. He was flirting with her. How brazen. She had to give him credit for having cajones.

He moved on to Rooster and then the rest of the team, shaking their hands in typical fashion. Rooster elbowed her teasingly. "He likes you," he whispered.

"I have a feeling he likes every female that moves."

Rooster let loose with a laugh but stopped himself when the

staunch man glanced back suspiciously. This Castro was not one to be trifled with.

They stood on the tarmac at the airport in Havana. She was already in love with Cuba. Flying over the Caribbean watching the water below turn myriad shades of blue, she'd been enchanted. As they stood there waiting for introductions to be completed, she took off her sweater, not needing it over her flowery sundress. A breeze whipped up and played with her big skirt and the pink can-can underneath. She held down her skirt at the same time she felt a sense of freedom in this balmy weather. She couldn't wait to slip into a swimsuit and jump into that aqua blue sea.

That Castro fellow excused himself, saying he would be in the front row of the game the next day. A bus arrived to take them to the National Hotel of Cuba, where an American guide awaited them. Dolly was surprised to learn that the opulent Spanish-style masterpiece was owned and operated by an American company. As it turned out, Cuba's President Batista was "in bed with" the U.S. government, that being Rooster's description, not the guide's. Cubans weren't even allowed to stay in this hotel, which catered exclusively to Americans who gambled in the casino and "enjoyed the hotel's other pleasures," as the guide said. Dolly figured that meant there was some hanky-panky going on but figured that wouldn't have anything to do with her and Rooster.

On the way to the room the two of them would share, she eyed exquisite chandeliers, carved mahogany furniture, dark wood coffered ceilings, Spanish tile floors, and brass accoutrements galore. In their room, she stepped out onto the balcony to take in the breadth and beauty of the view of the sea, accompanied by an ocean breeze that soothed her soul. She sucked in the ocean air, loving its fresh and salty smell tinged with the scent of the island's abundant yellow morning glories.

"Oh, Rooster, I love it here. Can we stay forever?" She turned around to find him standing in the middle of the room smiling. He came to her.

"I knew you'd love it here as much as I do. We might not be able to stay forever ..." he brushed an errant strand of hair off her cheek "... but there is something we can do that will last forever."

Dolly gasped when he got down on one knee, pulled a little velvet box out of his pocket, and opened it to reveal a large diamond ring.

"Dolly, will you marry me?"

"Yes! Yes, yes, yes, yes, yes." She reached down to throw her arms around his neck and they tumbled onto the floor. Laughing, they fell over each other getting up, but eventually they were standing and the ring sparkled on her finger.

It turned out there was a Catholic church nearby and a license wasn't required when enough cash was thrown around. Within two hours, they were wed.

Expecting a night of wedded bliss, Dolly was surprised when Rooster suggested they celebrate by gambling in the casino for a while. After that, he suggested they go to the bar. She was ready for some private hoochie-coochie time but wanted to please her groom. Once settled in the bar with El Presidente rum drinks at hand, Rooster excused himself and went into a back room. She figured the restrooms were back there. When he didn't come back after fifteen minutes, she started to worry. Maybe he was sick. Nervous, she finished her drink and ordered another. Fifteen more minutes went by before she realized that a lot of people came and went through that door in the back. Beautiful Cuban people, men and women. In fact, some of the most beautiful people she'd ever seen. Toned bodies, glossy black hair, and revealing attire abounded. It had started to dawn on her what might be going on back there when Rooster returned and sat down, excited as a kid at Christmas. And high on dope, she surmised from his glassy eyes.

"It's all set, sweetheart. The best wedding gift we could ever share."

"Oh? What is it?"

His smile was beatific. Those perfect snow-white teeth against his dark brown skin – she'd never forget that. "Two men for you and two girls for me. We'll be in separate rooms for an hour and then all together for another hour."

Dolly's lungs froze. She couldn't breathe.

"Dolly, honey? Are you okay? You've gone pale."

The anger that welled up within her frightened even her. She'd never known such fury before in her life. "No, I'm not okay," she seethed. "Whatever made you think that kind of thing would be okay with me? You didn't even ask me."

"Whoa. Wait a minute." His voice was curt, defensive. "Everybody knows you dated Wolff Garstonn, and everybody knows what he's like. I just assumed …"

"You 'just assumed'?" she cried. "Why in hell does everybody assume things about me without even asking?"

Rooster tried to grab her arm, but she yanked it away as she stood up so violently her chair toppled over. All eyes were on them.

He jolted up out of his chair and faced her. "Now, Dolly, wait. Don't make a scene." His ingratiating tone infuriated her even further. "Let's go to our room to talk about this."

"I want to make a scene and I don't want to go back to the room with you!" She shouted, the performer deep inside her enjoying embarrassing this asshole.

"Fine." Now he spoke between gritted teeth. "Do what you want, but I'm going back there." He turned his back on her and headed for that dreaded door.

Yanking the ring off her finger, she threw it at his back. It fell to the floor and stayed there. Dolly stared as he disappeared. A young woman, there with an older woman, neither who looked well-off, stooped down, picked up the ring, and held it out to Dolly. "Here, señorita, you can sell it and keep the dinero."

Dolly looked at the ring, looked at the girl, and said, "You keep it, honey. You sell it and keep the dinero. I don't want it."

As she tramped out of the bar, she heard applause erupt. She hadn't expected that here in Cuba, but it seemed she entertained people no matter where she went.

LAS VEGAS, 1995

"I FELT SO STUPID. Right then and there I determined that I was a damn-fool moron at picking men. I vowed never to get married again because I couldn't trust myself to pick a decent guy. I felt like I needed to tattoo my forehead that said, 'No orgies please.'"

The women nodded understanding and suggestions poured in.

"One prick at a time."

"No dickheads."

"How about 'one third leg for one gal.'"

"One set of balls only."

"Tea for two."

"One-man woman."

"Two to tango."

"Shlong along."

"That's a good one."

"Cock your pistol, take aim, and fire – away from me."

"Use your joy-stick with one chick."

"Or, 'Dip your stick in one chick'."

"Ha. Yeah, that's even better."

"Oh, I know, I know. 'No peckers, you feckers.'"

"How about this one? 'Down with cherry pickers.'"

"That looks like a penis, only smaller."

"No meanie weenies."

Tears of laughter rolled down their cheeks as the women's rapid-fire delivery veered out of control. Dolly dried her eyes with a cocktail napkin and looked at James. Thankfully, he was grinning.

"Oh, James, no offense or anything," Merry offered as she dried her eyes, too.

"None taken."

He didn't say anything else while they composed themselves, took sips of their drinks, and exhausted the last of their giggles.

"What were we talking about?" Dolly asked.

"You promised yourself you'd never marry again."

"Oh, yeah, that." She tittered.

"And you didn't, until Bill," Merry noted.

"Bill? I thought your husband was Otis," James said.

"Oh, he was," Merry explained, taking up her friend's story, which she knew well. "But first came Bill."

"I can't talk about him now. I'm hungry." Dolly craned her neck to look at a clock on the wall. "It's almost suppertime."

"One more question, if you don't mind." James tapped his pen on his notepad. "Did you ever see Fidel Castro again? Well, I guess two questions. Did you ever see Rooster again?"

"I went straight to the airport and got put on stand-by to fly home. While I waited, Fidel showed up. I was surprised. He'd obviously come just to talk to me. He said he'd heard that my 'el amigo' had disappointed me. That really surprised me because the bar scene had just happened a couple of hours earlier. When I told him that, he laughed. He said Havana wasn't a very big city, and he made it his business to know everything that went on there. He apologized that I'd had such a bad time in Cuba. He hoped I would come back and let him and the Cuban people provide me with a happier visit. I admit, I was totally charmed. When I was called to board, I started to kiss him on the cheek, but he turned his head and gave me a full-on kiss on the lips."

"Yeah, and she liked it," Ginger teased.

"I admit I did. He was so sweet to me, I was totally shocked later when he overtook the country and became a dictator hated by so many people. See? I didn't know how to pick a good man."

"Wow. What an incredible experience. What about Rooster?" James repeated his second question. "Did you ever see him again? Like when you went through a divorce, did you have to interact face-to-face?"

"No, I never saw him again. I read that he got married, which was interesting because I never bothered to divorce him. I don't know if he managed a divorce without my knowledge or not. The scuttlebutt in club dressing rooms was that he took an underage girl across state lines to have sex and the girl's daddy threatened to have him arrested if he didn't marry her. I ignored all that as much as possible and buried myself in my work for a long time. Now, how about we go to the diner and eat?"

It only took them fifteen minutes to get to the '50s Diner. It turned out they were all hungry, so no one dallied as they walked the short way there.

"I'm tellin' you, I can't wait to read this book." Betty sat with them at the big table, her shift having ended. She still wore her apron, and her tiara was still nested in her beehive. Apparently, that tiara represented more than a mere work prop for her, Dolly thought. It had become part of her persona. Dolly got a kick out of that.

They were all there – Dolly, Ginger, Merry, Annie, Layla, and James. Betty felt like a nice addition. Rosemary Clooney even sang "Sisters" in the background.

"I wish I coulda been a burly-que girl," Betty said as they waited for their meals. "Hard to believe now, but at one time I was quite the looker." She patted her helmet of hair to emphasize her point.

"I jus' didn't have the nerve to go public. But I had quite the routine I performed in private fer my beaus back home in Arkansas. One in particular. He musta loved it, because he went on to become one of the biggest muckety-muck politicians in Washington, D. of C."

"Well," James said dubiously, "the 'biggest' would be the President or Vice President or a Supreme Court judge or… "

"Uh huh. You've got the idea. And I've got pictures and letters to prove it."

Everyone stared at Betty.

The jukebox switched to Elvis singing "Love Letters," which serendipitously seemed to verify her claim.

"Maybe we should make Betty an honorary burly-que girl," Dolly suggested.

Everyone agreed.

"Betty," James said as he leaned over the table to get more personal, "if I can see those photos and letters tomorrow, I'd like to include you in our book. I could bring a contract. It pays $1,000 plus a small percent of profits."

Betty stiffened in surprise, then relaxed and smiled broadly. "Sure. I'd be honored."

"You have no trouble talking about someone who was famous?"

"Nah. No trouble at all." She waved a hand of dismissal. "Believe you me, he deserves whatever he gits."

"I'd like to hear your story right now, but I don't have anything for taking notes." James looked around, wishing he'd brought his backpack.

"Here." Betty pulled her order pad out of her pocket, took the pencil out of her hair, and slid them across the table. "Let's get started."

Six, Dolly realized. James had wanted 6 former exotic dancers to put into the book. Now he had them. It took an hour for him to be satisfied that he had everything he needed from Betty for now.

He made arrangements to come in the next day to witness the photos and letters, bring a contract and check, and chat some more if any questions came to mind.

Dolly watched in wonder. Betty exemplified the point Dolly had made earlier, that thing about assumptions. We can never assume anything about anyone, she thought. Here was a not-young waitress in a little diner who appeared to have a mundane life. Yet she'd had an affair with one of the most powerful men in the country. Until we get to know someone, she thought, we must remember that we don't know.

CHAPTER 13

"*O*kay, girls, line up right here in front of the mirror." Back at the hotel, Annie barked orders for what the rest of the women guessed was going to be a hair and makeup party.

James had been dismissed to go to his room, which he said was fine. He would spend the evening working on the book.

Annie's "big surprise" had included making the women get into their silk pajamas, which they all had because of their shopping spree a couple of days before, compliments of her illicit credit at the Bellagio and its stores. They'd invited Betty to this party, so Dolly loaned her a pair of PJs seeing that she'd bought three pairs and hadn't had a chance to wear two of them yet.

Then Annie had insisted they partake of a bottle of wine, which they'd brought with them into her master bathroom. Wine glasses lined the long marble countertop that held two brass sinks. A crystal chandelier in the middle of the ceiling provided plenty of light.

Now the women lined up as instructed, looking in the mirror. Layla, sexy even though needing to lean on her cane; Merry, thin and toned from years of yoga and healthy living; Annie, looking

123

younger than her years due to some excellent artificial assistance; Ginger, a tad overweight but perky as hell; Dolly, voluptuous and sensuous; and Betty, looking every bit like the former Corn Pone Queen they'd learned she had once been.

"Well, look at us. We are officially the six Burly-Q Girls!" Dolly whooped and raised her fists. "With a capital B and capital Q and capital G!"

The others joined in and the mood had been set. This party would be fun.

"Okay," Annie said as she picked up the big Dior bag she'd brought in that afternoon and set it on the counter. "Here's your surprise. Can you guess what we'll be doing? Let's call it 'TTT'."

A barrage of guesses ensued. "Tremendous something." "Tantalizing – I don't know." "Terrific time." "Knowing you, it's torture something or other." "Titillating?"

"Close!" Annie responded to "titillating". Burrowing into the bag, she pulled out a little black dress, a pair of white slacks, and a lacy bra and panty set. "Oops. I bought a few things for myself, too." She tossed those onto the floor and reached into the bag once more. "Here they are." She took out six small silk pouches and handed one to each woman.

Each looked inside her pouch.

"No." Ginger was aghast.

"Ha," Merry chuckled.

"I don't believe it." Dolly fingered hers.

"Well, these are my first." Layla stared at hers.

"What in hell are they?" Betty asked.

Annie pulled hers out and held up two little red sequined heart-shaped pyramids with a tassel hanging from the center of each one. "Pasties! It's 'Titty Twirling Time'! Ginger can teach us how to twirl the tassels."

"Where in the name of the Devil himself did you get these?" Dolly was more shocked than accusatory.

"Oh, I know the tailor at Dior. He made them for us. He's so sweet. Come on, off with our tops." She didn't even bother unbuttoning hers, instead pulling it off over her head and tossing it onto the floor with her new clothes. "See, they have little strips of paper on the back. Pull that off." She pointed to the backs. "There's sticky stuff to hold them on." She stripped the pieces of paper off hers and stuck them onto her nipples. Hands on hips, she looked at herself in the mirror. "Oh my god, these are so cute." She jiggled her chest. "Come on, what're you waiting for? Here this'll help." She pushed a button on a CD player that sat on a shelf behind them, and the iconic dancer song "The Stripper" played. Turning it up a bit, she left it low enough so they could still talk, too.

Dumbstruck, the others stared in the mirror at Annie's artificially enhanced but admittedly attractive breasts with their shiny pasties.

Merry, who practiced yoga every day in the nude anyway, gave up and shed her top. Betty was next, which surprised Dolly. Then Layla, who said, "Oh, what the hell. I'll never get another chance in this lifetime to do this." Ginger heaved a heavy sigh, took a swig of her wine, and said, "Okay. But don't laugh at my body." "Never," Dolly reassured her. Finally, Dolly gave in and got rid of her top, too.

They stuck on their little red hearts, then stood there staring in the mirror at their assortment of boobs that hung in a variety of configurations. Layla's breasts were full and hung halfway to her waist. Merry's were small and quite pert, but a few inches lower than they'd once been. Annie's boob job gave hers the look of an athletic forty-year-old. Ginger's were medium-sized and also making their way to her waist. Dolly's were large and making their own journey south. Betty's had already arrived.

"Mine look like a couple of pale zucchinis," Betty observed.

"Hmmm. The twins sure aren't where they used to be, not for most of us," Dolly noted. "When they say your breasts will sag when you get older, I used to think that meant they'd tip down a little bit. I didn't know that meant they'd slither underneath my skin in a race to see which one could hit my waist first."

"Want to see where they used to be? For just a second? Do this." Annie threw her arms up into the air at the same time she hopped up off both feet. For the split second that she came down her breasts stayed behind. For that brief moment they'd looked like the knockers of a twenty-two-year-old.

Merry tried it next, shouting "woo" as she hopped.

Watching in awe, one-by-one they jumped up like kids to see what used to be, except for Layla, whose knees couldn't take it. Instead, she served as cheerleader, egging them on as they repeated the move.

The giggling started at one end of the line and carried like a wave at a football game until all of them were laughing.

"Let's see," Dolly said, "there must be a chant to go with this. Um … 'My boobs ain't where they used to be …'" She hesitated as she tried to come up with something. "… but I don't care 'cuz I'm still me.'"

That generated a round of applause.

"How about this," Annie said. "'B-O-O …'" she paused "… B-S. I love my breasts, yes, yes yes!"

Hooting and hollering erupted along with more applause.

They made up hand movements to go with the cheer and pulled it off like college cheerleaders.

Finally, they decided it was time to get on with the task at hand. After all, this whole thing started so Annie could learn to twirl the tassels on her pasties.

"Come on, Ginger, let's roll," Annie coaxed.

"Crap, I can't believe I'm doing this." Ginger dropped her head into her hands.

"We used to be strippers, remember? This isn't anything compared to that," Annie said, egging her on.

"Come on," was the rallying cry from all quarters.

Ginger shook her head, but her cockeyed grin belied her delight. "Okay, here's the deal. You can't just shake your chest. You have to rotate your shoulders and slightly pump your legs at the same time. I haven't done it since forever, so I don't know if it'll work, but here goes."

She demonstrated with a move that only managed to bop her breasts up and down.

"This sounds a lot like a belly dancing move. Without a bare chest and pasties, of course. Let me try." Layla gave it a go and got half circles out of the tassels on her pasties.

Ginger said, "Well-done, girl." Then she tried again. This time the tassels on her pasties made three full circles, but in the same direction. "Wait. I think I've got it this time." She tried again and the tassels spun in opposite directions, one clockwise and the other counterclockwise.

The accolades became raucous. Annie turned up the music to blasting level. It took a lot of tries, a lot of laughter, and a lot of wine, but eventually everybody could twirl their pasties at least in the same direction while Ginger and Layla mastered opposite directions.

Annie grabbed a tube of lipstick and wrote "Burly-Q Girls rule!" on the mirror in giant red letters. When she turned up the music full tilt, they went to town giving it every bit of performance shtick they'd ever had. They howled to the music, whipped their fannies to and fro, and twirled those sequined pasties. This was the most fun they'd had in …

"What in hell is going on here?" A man's voice bellowed through the room.

"Holy shit!

"Damn."

"What in hell?"

"Whoa."

"Who the fuck is that?"

Everyone scrambled to put on their tops now that a strange man stood in the doorway. Everyone except Annie, who calmly reached over to turn off the music. As nonchalantly as if she were walking down the street fully clothed, she turned around and faced the man, her breasts with their sequined pasties pointing straight at him, daring him to try to look away.

"Hello, *mom*," the man snarled.

Annie thrust her hands onto her hips, puffed out her chest, and said, "Girls, meet Lemuel Jones Junior, my mother-fucking, cock-sucking, prick of a stepson."

"It's good to see you, too, mommy dearest." Sarcasm dripped from his lips.

Dolly studied the man. Medium height, not bad looking, maybe sixty, in a conservative suit and tie. He looked ... stuffy, she decided. A bully. Probably spoiled rotten growing up with all that money in the family.

"Huh. If I really did have you for a son," Annie snarked, "it'd make me believe in infanticide. You need to leave. This is a private party."

"I can see that. And what a party it is. But, you see, it's over. I've informed management that your credit has been canceled. They've given me the privilege of kicking you out. Now. All of you, get out of here."

"Grandma? What's going on?" Malika showed up behind the man and inched her way around him to protectively go to her grandmother's side. "Why is everyone in the bathroom with this stranger?"

"It's all right, dear," Layla reassured her. "We need to leave, is all."

"I'm not going anywhere." Annie stood her ground.

Everyone looked at her, looked at him, and looked back at her.

"Yes, you are," he hissed.

"You can't make me."

"Oh, yes, I can." This Lemuel Jones Junior tromped into the room, scooped up his stepmother, threw her over his shoulder, and turned to go. He had no idea what a mistake he'd made.

His cargo and five attackers pummeled him, shouting at him to let go of Annie. He had no choice, if he wanted to save his family jewels, other than to put her down. He straightened his lapels, smoothed his thinning hair, declared he'd be back with a manager and security guards, and stomped away in a red-faced rage.

James came to the rescue.

Dolly hated to admit that she saw him as a knight in shining armor because she liked to think she could always save herself, and she could, but it was a relief when he showed up as they were packing. When they called him in his room and explained their plight, he arranged for Champs Enterprises to pay for a room for each of them. Nobody had to leave the hotel.

For Dolly, Ginger, and Merry, it didn't take long to pack up their new couture clothes in their new designer luggage. Layla and Malika had only brought one bag each, so they were good to go. Betty hadn't brought anything except the clothes on her back and her purse.

Then there was Annie. She refused to budge. Sitting on the side of her bed with her arms crossed under her pastied but otherwise bare breasts, she wasn't going anywhere of her own accord. Dolly tried talking to her, to no avail. At the very least, she attempted to talk the stubborn woman into putting on her pajama top.

But Annie refused, sitting like a boulder, inert and immovable.

Her stepson reappeared with a hotel manager and two husky security guards, who picked her up as if she were a statue, carried her to the elevator, and deposited her in her new room. She remained stone still and stone silent. They sat her on the bed the same way she'd been before.

Dolly and Merry had followed. When the men left, Annie thawed. "Well, that was ridiculous," was all she said.

"We brought your things." Dolly and Merry each had a giant roller bag at hand, plus more garments in hand. "Layla and Malika are gathering up your shoes and bathroom stuff, and Betty and Ginger are checking around for anything else that might be yours. "Divide and conquer, we decided. James is working on finding us a room where we can all meet tomorrow to finish the book." Dolly did her best to sound reassuring.

"That penthouse sure was fun while it lasted," Merry said, looking around the nice but typical hotel room they stood in now. "Thank you for giving us the opportunity to stay there. It was a real treat. And for all the nice things we bought, too."

"That's right," Dolly agreed. "We'll never get a chance to do any of that again. You may have started out doing it just to get back at your stepson, but you ended up doing some very nice things for us anyway. Thank you."

Annie looked up at them with doleful eyes. With her shoulders slumped and her back humped, she almost looked pathetic. But Dolly couldn't quite go there yet.

The other women showed up with more of Annie's belongings, then everyone thanked their host for the pasties, saying the "pastie party" had been a blast. Ginger, Layla, and Malika showered her with thanks for the penthouse stay, with Ginger remembering to add the things she'd bought, too. Betty added, "Annie, honey, I had a riotously good time."

At first Annie glared at them like a rag doll. But suddenly, she came to life. "We did have fun, didn't we?"

Everyone nodded and echoed agreement.

"As scary as it was to have your stepson show up out of nowhere," Merry said, "the look on his face when he saw what we were doing, well, that almost made it worthwhile."

"He did look horrified, didn't he?" Annie smirked.

"Totally discombobulated," Dolly said.

"Well," Annie added, "at least we have that."

They all said good night. It had been a long, hard day.

Dolly told Betty to go ahead and keep the pajamas – they'd all stayed in their PJs while switching rooms – and Betty gave her a hug in return. They parted at the elevator, as Betty's room was on another floor. After she was gone, Dolly started back to her room, which happened to be next to Annie's.

Annie shot out her door like a rocket. Thank heaven, she'd put on her pajama top. "The Bentley! I have to go see if that motherfucker got my car!" Running to the elevator, she punched the button over and over. "Come on, come on, come on. I've got to get down there."

When the doors opened to two Japanese businessmen, who looked quizzically at the two women in pajamas but then shrugged, as if accepting that this must be one more strange American custom, Annie flew inside with Dolly right behind her. Annie assaulted that button, too, and swore when the elevator moved "like molasses in January."

At the lobby, she squeezed through the elevator doors before they were even fully open and ran outside to the valet parking stand. Dolly caught up as Annie pulled on her hair and urgently tried to find the young man who had her car hidden away. He appeared, and Annie grabbed him by the shoulders.

"Is my car still safe? Did someone try to take it?" she asked, frantic.

He stared at her for a moment, then shook his head. "Why no, Mrs. Jones. Nobody knows where it is but me. It's okay."

"Where is it?" Annie seemed to realize she was practically accosting the kid and let go of his body.

He looked chagrined. "Well, I let my grandpa keep it in his garage. He isn't driving it or anything. He just likes looking at it. He's been polishing it every day. He loves to make it shine."

"Oh my god, I love you. And I love your grandpa. You tell him that. Thank you so much. I'll need it tomorrow. You'll be here, right?" When they learned he'd be working a double shift the next day and would be there all day and evening, Annie finally relaxed. "Okay, like I promised, I'll give you a nice tip before I leave."

"Mrs. Jones, that doesn't even matter. This has made my grandpa so happy it's been worth it."

"You mean you don't want money?"

"Nah. That's fine."

"Well, I'll give it to you anyway."

When she and Dolly went back inside, Annie said, "What in hell is wrong with young people these days? He doesn't want money? Pfft. I just don't understand this younger generation."

Dolly didn't say anything, but she was pretty sure this younger generation would never understand Annie, either. She was still grappling with that herself.

CHAPTER 14

"**W**ere there ever times when you felt lonely? Being on the road as much as you were, there must have been times when you missed being at home." James threw out the question at random, having given up on orderly interviewing.

They sat in a "salon," a room of the hotel set up for small meetings with comfy sofas and armchairs. Coffee mugs rimmed the coffee table and a platter in the center offered a variety of yummy donuts.

"I was never lonely," Annie offered. "I was always so busy I didn't have time to think about it."

"Yeah, let's be honest here, Annie." Ginger seemed to be in a testy mood on this morning. "You were busy plying your trade off-stage."

Yup, Dolly thought, that girl needed more coffee.

Annie didn't flinch. "Yes. I did. And I'm not ashamed of that. I had a lot of boyfriends, and I made a lot of money. Without that I never would have met my pookie."

"Good god, did you actually always call him Pookie?" Ginger goaded her.

"Yes. You're just jealous because you never had a pookie."

"Okay, ladies," James intervened, "let's get back to the question. Annie, you were never lonely on the road. Good. Who else wants to chime in?" He looked hopefully from face to face.

Dolly watched as Ginger's blood boiled for a moment; then she calmed down. Dolly hoped she'd remembered her blood pressure medication that morning.

"I missed my daughter something awful when I traveled," Merry offered. "I didn't start yoga and meditation instruction until she was 12. A year later I started doing Reiki. Before that, when I was still dancing for a living, I didn't travel much. I worked in clubs close to home, mostly in Boulder and Denver, but when I did travel, it felt like my heart was being ripped apart. She had a great sitter, so I wasn't worried about that. I just couldn't wait to get back to her – to my real life. I was so happy when my businesses built up to the point that I didn't have to dance anymore."

"I know what you mean about starting a new business," Layla said. "I can't say I was happy not to have to dance, because I loved it, but it was a relief when I started making enough money on my day job that I didn't have to rely on dancing alone to support my family. At first after my husband died and I had four kids to feed, I only had my dancing. I had no idea what else I could do. I had no job experience at all. Then a friend suggested I try selling real estate. I gave it a shot and was surprised that I was good at it. But it took a few years to build up that business to the point that I could trust it to take care of us. After that, I was able to dance only when I wanted to for enjoyment. I did that for a long time. I miss it." She patted the ever-present cane that leaned up against her chair.

James nodded at Layla and looked at Ginger.

"Well, I liked dancing. My only problem with travel was when I was married for a while and he turned out to be a scumbag. Every time I hit the road, I figured he was screwing some bitch back home. When I came home early one time, I caught him in our bed in our house – my bed, my house – going at it so hard they didn't even hear me come home. I had to turn on the overhead light and scream to get their attention. Needless to say, that marriage was over. Then traveling became a way of soothing my sorrows. Not long after that, though, the truth is I felt like I wasn't good enough at it anymore, and I knew it was time to quit. Besides, I gained a little weight …" She patted her small melon of a belly. "… and didn't look the part anymore, either." She picked up her mug and took a sip of her morning brew.

"Pfft. You still look cute."

Every head turned to stare at Annie. She'd just complimented Ginger, the woman she'd tormented when they were young women, the very woman who now seemed hell-bent on tormenting her back.

Annie shrugged. "Well, she is. Don't you ever let anybody tell you anything different, Ginger."

Ginger glared at her nemesis, suspicious of this dame who now seemed like a stranger in their midst. She had no response to the shocking comment as she gulped down the rest of her coffee.

Dolly was skeptical, as well. Annie was acting awfully chirpy considering the events of the night before. That widow, who clearly had no desire to mourn the loss of her husband but instead mourned the loss of his money, was up to something and there was no telling what manner of trouble it might be.

"Annie, that's a nice thing for you to say," James said. "And it's true. Now, Dolly, what about you? Were you ever lonely on the road? I know you had the longest career of anyone here, and you traveled the most. What was that like for you?"

Dolly had been listening to the others at the same time she'd been formulating her answer. She'd decided to be brutally honest. If anyone read this book who was thinking about life on the road, they deserved to know the truth.

"I never felt lonely on the road. In fact, when I came home, I couldn't wait to get out there again. I felt like a gypsy. A citizen of the world. The entire Earth was my domain. Oh, I loved my little craftsman-style house in Detroit, but only saw it as a stopping point. That was until I met Bill. He was a manager at the Ford plant, the very place my parents had always wanted me to work. Oh my god, he was handsome. We met in a club where I was dancing, of course, and right away there was a ginormous attraction." She chuckled and shook her head at the recollection. "I was thirty-seven years old, sick of dating, and ready for love with one man, that's for sure. It wasn't long before he moved into my house with me.

"I must admit, that was a relief. He made good money and had no trouble paying the bills. He took care of things while I was on the road. He treated me like a queen. We were madly in love. We said 'I love you' all the time. Best of all, we laughed a lot." Lost in thought for a moment, she went back to that time and place in her mind. No one intruded on her thoughts, letting her return to the past. She came back to say, "We would dance to music on the radio. He would sit on the couch and watch me practice a new routine in the living room. Our life in the bedroom was fantastic. I had a perfect life.

"I called him often from the road, but sometimes got so wound up in what I was doing and who I was meeting, I'd forget for a couple of days. Then things started to change. He asked me to cut down on my schedule, to stay home more. We didn't need the money, he reminded me. I spent most of my money on costumes and clothes and traveling, anyway. I didn't need all of that. He wasn't asking me to quit altogether; he simply wanted more time together. He said he yearned for my warm body in bed next to him at night. You see, he was the one who was lonely, not me. Our whole life was set up for me but not for him.

"I told him I'd think about it but, honestly, I didn't. That went on for three or four years. He was very patient. Finally, one day as

I was packing for yet another tour, he told me he couldn't live like that anymore. He gave me an ultimatum. Cut down on my schedule or he would need to leave. He wanted a wife, not a casual visiting lover."

"Were you two married?" James asked.

"No. That was another problem. He'd got the license long before, but I never found the time for a wedding. That was another stick in his craw.

"My response to his ultimatum was to give him a big kiss and tell him to calm down. I'd think about it. Really, I would, I said. Then I went on my merry way. I was excited because I was doing a three-week tour in the Philippines. I'd never been there before. I'd be meeting President Marcos and his wife Imelda. It would be an exciting adventure. I was always up for adventures."

She stared out the window.

"But," she finally went on with her story, "in the end, I became the lonely one."

DETROIT, Michigan, 1973

DOLLY HOPPED out of the cab and stood there in the snow, staring at her house. It confused her. Every time she'd come home before in December, Bill had the house decorated for Christmas. Colorful lights strung along the roofline of the front porch, garlands on the railing, and a beautiful wreath on the door – none of which was there this year. The Christmas tree that usually sat inside at the front window was missing, too. There were no lights on inside. The place sat there looking cold and barren. Almost ... abandoned.

She scanned the yard. The driveway and sidewalk weren't shoveled and were covered in a foot of snow. Others houses on the block looked festive and warm, with all the symbols of the holiday she'd expected here. Their walkways and driveways were shoveled to clear the way for human activity.

The cab driver had unloaded her three huge suitcases from his trunk – she'd shipped all her costumes home, as they didn't fit into baggage like this – and he stood there, clearly wondering what to do next. Reaching into the backseat to retrieve her purse and the large shopping bag full of shoe boxes – Imelda Marcos had taken her shoe shopping – she struggled to breathe. Surely all of this wasn't what it seemed.

"Miss O'Dare, would ya like me tah take these tah yer front door, or is there a side door ya use instead?" The cabbie sounded solemn, the antithesis of his jolly mood driving in from the airport. He'd read the situation at this house, and he knew it wasn't good.

"The front door, please."

Together they trudged through the snow and up the porch steps. Dolly turned the doorknob, but it was locked. She froze. Bill always had it unlocked because he was always waiting for her on the other side.

"Oh. Oh, I need to find my keys." She set down the shopping bag and rummaged through her purse, avoiding the look of pity on the cabbie's face. "Ah. Here they are." She fumbled with the lock, but finally got the door open.

He set her luggage and big shopping bag inside, and then took off his fur-lined bomber hat, the kind of warm headgear men had been wearing since the war. He held the hat at his chest. "Miss O'Dare, ya gonna be okay? I mean, it's Christmas Eve and all. My missus makes a fine Christmas dinner. Would ya like tah join us? We've got plenty, I'm sure."

Dolly studied the little man who looked like he didn't have a pot to piss in. He pitied her. She couldn't fathom it – her, the famous, world-renowned, globe-trotting star. Yet he pitied her.

Her heart melted in gratitude that someone on this earth cared that she was alone on Christmas Eve.

"Thank you so much. No, I'm fine. Really. I'll be meeting friends later on," she lied, doing her best to fake a smile.

She took cash out of her purse for cab fare plus a fat tip and handed it to him.

"Why, thank ya. That's very generous. Merry Christmas, Miss O'Dare. God bless ya." He stuffed the bills into his pocket, put on his hat, and turned to go. He was halfway out the door when a thought occurred to her.

"Wait." He turned back to her. "Do you have children?"

He tossed out a smile that displayed a missing incisor. "Yes, miss. Five. They're the joy of my life."

Dolly reached into her purse and pulled out more cash, not even bothering to count it. "Here, get them something extra special for Christmas." She held it out to him, but he hesitated to take it.

"Oh, Miss O'Dare, ya've already given me plenty. I don't think ..."

"Here. I insist. Take it. Tell your children they have a very special dad."

Haltingly, he took the money. "Thank ya. This means a lot tah us. Thank ya."

Once he left, Dolly closed the door and strained to breathe as she flicked on a light and surveyed the living room. She shivered in the cold, as the heat had obviously been turned down. Aware that her shoes dripped snow onto the carpet, she shucked them off. She was struck by the big things she'd expected that were absent, like a Christmas tree, a burning fireplace, carols playing on the record player, and the aroma of Christmas dinner wafting in from the kitchen. Bill was a great cook and loved preparing holiday meals. Then she noticed the little things. Every single item that had been Bill's was gone. The pack of Marlboros that always sat on the end table beside his recliner. His reading glasses. The book he'd been reading. He was always reading a book. His slippers beside the chair. The blanket he kept at hand in case he got cold while watching TV. The picture of the two of them that he'd put on the mantle.

She stood in the middle of the room not knowing what to do next. She dared not go into the bedroom to find his side of the closet empty and his favorite pillow missing from his side of the bed. That would destroy her.

Dolly O'Dare, who only three days earlier had performed at a gala event in front of hundreds of cheering fans at the invitation of the president of a country, was all by herself. The thrill of dancing for that audience had been exhilarating, a kind of high she could never replicate in any other way. But now those fans were nowhere in sight. No one, in fact, was in sight. Not even her Bill. She was totally and utterly alone.

In a spate of fury, she kicked the bag of shoe boxes, sending designer footwear flying across the room. She'd thought those bits of molded leather had been so important and couldn't wait to show them to Bill. Now she loathed their very existence.

Bereft beyond belief, she crumbled onto the floor and sobbed.

CHAPTER 15

*L*as Vegas, 1995

DOLLY HEAVED a sigh and swiped at a moist eye. "That was one of the lowest points of my life."

"Let's take a break," James suggested. "I'm sorry if that question was upsetting."

"Oh, I'm okay. It's my own stupidity back then that hits so hard. There was a note on the kitchen table. It said he'd realized he and I were never going to have a real life together, a marriage. He wanted that and had found someone else who wanted the same thing. It was surreal. He'd left a stack of paid bills so I'd know who had to be paid in the future to keep the house running. I did a terrible job of that, and a couple of months later came home to a freezing cold house because I'd forgotten to pay the heating bill. His note said he'd had the oil changed in my car and it was full of gas, safe in the garage. There was stuff for sandwiches in the fridge. It was so matter-of-fact it broke my heart.

"I asked myself a thousand times why I let that happen. I'd been so dead set on doing everything my way. I totally took him for granted. Why, when I loved Bill more than life itself, had I been so unwilling to compromise? Why had I allowed my need to dance destroy the love of my life? Part of it was a craving for fame, but it was more than that. I felt like this one thing was my only way of giving back to the world, of making people happy. But I let that destroy the happiness of someone I loved, and my own." She took a breath and drank her coffee.

"Tell him what happened a coupla years later," Ginger suggested.

"Yeah, honey, that's the amazing part," Merry encouraged.

"You two go ahead."

"She danced for a couple more years, but her heart wasn't in it anymore," Merry explained.

"Wait," James interceded. "You quit two years after that?" Dolly nodded. "Was it a hard decision to finally give it up?"

"No. Surprisingly, the night came when I knew without a doubt the time had come."

HARBOR SPRINGS, Michigan, 1975

CAB CALLOWAY and his band played for over an hour, their jazz, bebop, and swing whipping up the energy in the room to a fevered pitch. The dance floor was packed with revelers, yet everyone seemed to find enough room to jive with wild abandon. Bodies bumped into bodies and legs flew into the air as women were thrown onto their partners' hips. Women were dressed to the nines but stoles, hats, gloves, and belts had been left at their tables. Men had started out in their customary suits and ties, but jackets and neckwear were long gone, while shirt collars had been unbuttoned and sleeves had been rolled up. A pile of shoes in the corner indicated that many of them had shucked the impediment of footwear.

The place smelled of cologne, cigarette smoke, sweat, and booze. The haze of smoke formed a sensuous scrim that filled the room, giving everyone a mysterious allure.

Dolly felt ecstatically happy. This was her world, her heaven on earth, and these were her people.

It was "Maid and Butler Night Out" at the Golden Horseshoe Supper Club in Harbor Springs, Michigan, one of her favorite venues. A resort establishment, for six nights a week it catered to wealthy white summertime residents, including those who owned resplendent homes and those who came in on their yachts. But Monday night was the night when the "help" had the night off, and that was the night when all good hell broke loose. Maids might be quiet at work and butlers might be stoic on the job but let them out for a night of fabulous music and topnotch entertainment, and they knew, better than anyone else on earth Dolly believed, how to have fun.

She lived for these nights.

They were black folks with a few Caribbeans. The few white people in the room enjoyed watching from their tables.

The evening started with the band playing while people entered and settled in. Even though it was a supper club, few Monday nighters ordered a full meal. They'd already eaten their own much less expensive fare and weren't here for that. Instead, they ordered dessert and drinks.

An hour after opening, Dolly did her first performance of the evening. When she reached the second part of her act where she invited people up onto the stage, it overflowed with fabulous dancers. Then she jumped down into the middle of the dance floor where everyone joined in. As much as she loved being the center of attention, being lost in the middle of this gang filled her with joy.

Cab, known as Mr. Hi-de-ho, took the mic and started to scat his signature song while dancing his famous gliding backstep. "Hi-de-hi-de-hi-de-ho …" The roar of the crowd as they joined in felt like it'd lift the roof. Everyone knew all the words and sang at the top of their lungs.

An hour later, happily exhausted, folks sat down and ordered more drinks as the band took a break. A young waitress, a white college student who Dolly thought far too naïve to be working in this place, brought a large glass of iced water and two-fingers of bourbon into the dressing room for her. The girl had never looked comfortable in the chorus girl costume waitresses had to wear, with the Golden Horseshoe having an old west theme. Designed by the same company that did the Playboy bunny costumes, Dolly knew those getups must be ungodly uncomfortable. A cinched-waist, high-on-the-thigh, low-at-the bodice number, with a large bow and tail of fabric in the back and a plumed headdress, the thing must weigh a ton. They wore black net stockings and a red garter to top off the bottom.

She thanked the girl and turned back to her mirror to fix her melting makeup. She mixed vanilla extract with pancake foundation, as it wasn't possible to find foundation that matched her skin color.

"Miss O'Dare," the waitress said shyly.

"Yes?"

"I want you to know how much I enjoy your show. I can't imagine having enough courage to do such a thing. I think you're wonderful. And I'm having the time of my life tonight."

"Really? How old are you?" Dolly didn't turn around, instead addressing the girl in her mirror.

"I turned 21 the day before I started work here for the summer."

Dolly turned to face her. "Ah, and this is the last night for the summer, and then you're back to college. What do you plan to do when you graduate?"

"I … I don't know."

Dolly thought it odd that the girl had spent three years in college and still had no clue where her life was headed. She'd known since she was 16.

"Well, I'm sure it'll come to you." She wasn't sure at all but wanted to be encouraging. "I'm glad you're having a good time."

The girl left, and Dolly felt as if something had been left unsaid. Something unfinished.

Back in the club, the band started up. She performed another number on stage, but when it came time to invite others up again, she paused. There was that insecure waitress, working away in the back of the room.

"Excuse me!" she shouted into the mic. "Miss. The waitress in the back." The young woman looked up, surprised, and pointed at herself questioningly. "Yes, you. Put down that tray and come on up here, honey." The waitress shook her head "no", but the audience wasn't having it. Two men popped up to offer an arm on each side of her, and they playfully squired her up onto the stage. The girl stood there in a stupor.

"What's your name?"

"Um … Lucinda."

"Lucinda. Hmmm, Lucinda Baby Boo, how about we work on your shyness?"

The crowd clapped enthusiastically.

Lucinda, who Dolly had just dubbed "Baby Boo," looked stricken.

"Come on. Take my hand and follow me." Dolly nodded at the band, and they started out nice and slow. "Step, step, step, like this." Dolly did a little shuffle and the clumsy girl did her best to do it, too. The audience clapped again. "Now this." Dolly stepped it up, let go of the girl's hand, and twirled.

Lucinda appeared to relax a little and managed a nice twirl. The crowd continued to show their appreciation. The girl grinned out at them.

"Okay, now this," Dolly instructed, elegantly striding across the stage.

Lucinda followed.

"Shimmy." Dolly shook her body. She wore a little outfit the size of a swimsuit, with bangles that glistened in the light as she shook.

Lucinda hesitated, apparently decided "what the hell", and performed it pretty well.

"Now, don't worry, I'm not going to ask you to strip, but how about we get rid of that big old silly skyscraper on your head?"

Lucinda smiled, happy to get rid of the thing. Dolly helped her unpin it, and they cast it to the floor. More clapping and hollering ensued.

"Now, your high heels."

The girl kicked them off.

"And, to make your audience happy, take off your garter, like this." Dolly pretended she wore a garter and seductively inched the imaginary thing down her leg, twirled it on her finger, and cast it into the crowd.

Now Lucinda got into it, mimicking her perfectly and tossing her real garter out to the audience. That was met with more than generous praise.

The music quickened, others joined them onstage, Dolly jumped off the stage to go back into the crowd, and Lucinda's hand was taken as she became mired in the melee of dancing. Dolly delighted in thinking she'd helped that girl come out of her shell, and that her roomful of friends had been so accepting and welcoming of someone who seemed misplaced.

Later that night, after the club closed, she, the band, and club workers relaxed on a remote beach on Little Traverse Bay to say their goodbyes for the summer. Dolly sat alone on a small hill of soft white sand watching sparks from their bonfire pirouette up to meet the stars in the sky. It was a spectacular summer night, one that was perfect for the decision she contemplated, as if the universe spoke to her.

Cab came over and sat beside her, offering her a hit on his joint. She took it, inhaled a few times, and handed it back to him.

"What's on your mind, Dolly O'Dare?"

"What makes you think something's on my mind?" Her tone was jovial.

"Well, let me see. We've known each other since I was wearing zoot suits and you were a skinny kid just learning the business. We've ended up at the same clubs – what? – two or three times a year for all those years. I think I know what you're thinking, 'cuz I'm thinking the same thing." He finished his reefer and stubbed it into the sand.

She nodded. "Yes. Tonight was perfect. The last night at a beautiful club with you and your band, and a crowd that can never be beat. I've been dancing for over thirty years. It's time for me to end it now in the best way possible rather than waiting for it all to go downhill."

Cab nodded knowingly. "I'd have slowed down a lot by now if I hadn't played the ponies too much over the years. It's hard to admit, isn't it, that our best show days are behind us? I still love performing, but my Cotton Club days are over."

"Yes. It is hard to admit. But it sure has been wonderful, hasn't it?"

"Uh huh, it has. We've had good lives, Dolly O'Dare, despite some rough times. Not many people get to experience everything we have. Not everybody gets to do what they love to do."

They sat in silence, each lost in thought, watching others chatting by the fire, wading in the bay, and staring at the night sky. Then Dolly spied the waitress, Lucinda, standing alone on the side, hands in jeans' pockets, watching the flames.

"Baby Boo!" The girl looked up. "Come on over here." Dolly patted the sand beside her.

Lucinda came over and plopped down. "Hi. I wanted to stop by to say thank you for such a fun time. I've never done anything like that, and I loved it." She smiled brilliantly.

"Well, good. That's real good, isn't it, Cab?"

"I'll say. You did a fine job. You can be proud of yourself."

"How did you ever end up working at the Golden Horseshoe?" Dolly asked. "I mean, we love it, but it doesn't seem like your kind of place. You never seemed comfortable in that costume, for one thing."

"That is the darndest thing I've ever had to wear. I hated it. It was torture. But it was the only job I could find for the summer, and I have to work."

"Well, you could learn to take your clothes off like I do. Then you wouldn't have to worry about it," Dolly teased, supposing she pushed the girl a bit more out of her comfort zone. But Baby Boo surprised her.

"I would if I thought I had the body for it. No, all I want to do is travel, and I can't figure out a career where I'll get to do that. My college counselor says I have to be a teacher."

Cab leaned forward to look at her. "Do you want to be a teacher?"

"Fuck, no."

"Good for you," Cab said, grinning. "Be honest about it."

"How about being a stewardess?" Dolly suggested. "They travel all the time."

"I know, and I think I'd love that. But I don't know how to get a job doing that."

"Well, the first thing you have to do is leave small town Michigan and go to Chicago," Cab offered. "I've heard tell that airlines have offices there where they hire people. My friend's daughter got hired by TWA there."

"I don't have any money. I have to go right back to waitressing at a place in my college town when classes start next week."

"You don't need money, not if you're determined enough," Dolly instructed. "Hell, we all started out with nothing, and look at us."

"Call long-distance information," he advised. "Find a number for TWA in Chicago. Call them up. Ask for an application. They'll send you one. Fill it out real nice. Send it back. They'll call you for an interview. Maybe they'll even send you a ticket to fly to Chicago. Or drive if you have to."

"If you're scared to drive to the city, tough. Get over it," Dolly insisted. "Maybe you can sweet talk some boy into driving you in. You got a boyfriend?"

"Nah. I had one, but he's in the army in Korea and told me he's living with a mamasan. So I guess we're not going together anymore."

"Do you know what a 'mamasan' is?" Cab wanted to know.

"Nope. But I can guess."

"Well, take the bus if you must," Dolly said.

"Yeah, I'll have to, because my old junker of a Beetle would never make it."

"Okay. Bus it is. Can you figure that out?"

"Yes. There's a bus station by my campus. I can ask them."

"Good," Cab said. "Then in the interview all you have to do is be your sweet self. You'll get hired on the spot, I'd bet anything."

Dolly threw him a look. He didn't need to be betting on anything.

"My college counselor never told me any of this," Lucinda

groaned. "Geez. I think I can do it." She brightened and stood up. "Well, I don't want to bother you anymore. Thank you so much. I'm going to do this. And, Dolly, I want you to know that tonight you did more than help me have fun. You helped me feel more like myself than I have since I was a kid. Thank you."

She threw them a wave and started to walk away.

"Hey, wait!" Dolly hollered. "Give me a call to let me know how it goes. Cab, you got anything I can write on?"

He pulled reefer paper and a pen out of his pocket. Dolly wrote down her phone number and handed it over.

"Here you go, Baby Boo. You give me call. Promise?"

"I promise."

"And remember," Cab added, "follow your heart. Do what you want to do. You can make it. If we could, you can too."

She nodded thoughtfully. "Thank you. Thank you both so much."

As she trotted away, Cab said, "I swear she's walking more confidently than she did before."

Dolly watched and had to agree. "That seals the deal. My work as an 'exotic dancer' is done. I've spent thirty years making people happy and I've changed a young woman's life. There's nothing left for me to do."

They both chuckled, and then went back to watching the night unfold before them, each profoundly content to simply sit quietly in the presence of an old friend.

LAS VEGAS, 1995

"SHE CAME HOME from that gig and called Balls to tell him she was retiring," Ginger said. "She was fifty and had been dancing for over thirty years. There was a big article about it in the *Detroit News* the week she quit the road and started a new job as hostess at a jazz club."

"There's a knock at her door at lunchtime one day that week …" Merry picked up the story "… and wouldn't you know, it's Bill. He brought flowers, a big gift box, and a homemade chocolate cake, her favorite, that he'd made himself."

"Wait. You let him in after what he'd done to you?" Annie seemed baffled.

"Yes. Of course." Dolly shrugged. "I still loved him. And I understood why he'd left me." She nodded at Ginger and Merry to continue.

"She fixed lunch, they ate cake, and he told her it turned out he had never been happy living with that other woman. He never married her. He'd always missed Dolly. Then she opened her present, and he'd brought her a beautiful black hat with a great big wide brim." Merry circled her hands two feet out from her head to illustrate. "Very sophisticated. She loved that hat."

Dolly became pensive. "Yes, it was such a great gift because he knew how much I love hats. He hadn't ever bought me clothes before because I always bought so many for myself, so that made that hat seem especially personal. Go ahead, tell the rest."

"Well," Ginger continued, "they ended up in the rack, of course, and when they were done, they were lying there laughing and smoking cigarettes."

"Yes. He always lit two at the same time and gave one to me. It was a sweet gesture. Sexy as hell, too," Dolly took up her own story. "We were smoking and talking about how much we'd missed each other, and all of a sudden he gasped and grabbed his chest. He died of a heart attack right there in my arms."

Dolly paused and no one interceded until Merry solemnly finished the tale for her. "She called an ambulance right away and did everything she could to save him, but he was gone."

"I wore the hat to his funeral," Dolly added, concluding the story.

"Dolly, I'm so sorry that happened to you," James said. "Let's take that break after all."

CHAPTER 16

"*A*re you okay?" James asked.

"Oh yeah, it just gets to me sometimes, even after all these years. Especially since Otis is gone now, too."

Dolly sat on a bench out front taking in the exquisite fountains that were the Bellagio's calling card. The giant gushers performed extravaganzas day and night, shooting towers of water up into the air in a spectacle like none she'd ever seen before. Out here near them, she could feel their refreshing residual mist. The sound of the cascading water soothed her.

James sat down beside her. "Did you ever see her again? That college kid. Lucinda."

That caused a softening of her face. "Oh, my, yes. I'm a second mama to her and she's the daughter I never had. She called when she got a job at TWA. She's traveled the world. Married a pilot. Has two kids and grandkids." She nudged his shoulder with hers, indicating her pleasure. "We see each other every year. She's very good to me. I know she'd give me money, if I asked, which is why I'll never ask."

Now he nudged her. "Are you going to be okay finishing up today?"

"Oh my, yes. We're going to talk about sex next, right? That'll be fun. That's the best way to lift my spirits."

"Good. Well, right now the rest of the crew is inside talking about going to the diner for lunch. I offered to take all of you to lunch here, where we have some of the best restaurants in Vegas, but they want the diner. Is that okay with you?"

"Sure. That place has become like a second home to us. Betty's working today, so we get to see her, too. You know, she's officially one of the Burly-Q Girls now."

James stood up and offered a hand. She took it, and they went back inside.

Over lunch at the diner, Layla talked about how much fun Malika was having at the impersonators' conference. The young woman hadn't decided if she liked Elvis or Superman best but might be leaning toward Elvis. Layla also reminded everyone that her granddaughter was belly dancing on stage that evening and they were invited. They all agreed they wouldn't miss it for anything.

After lunch, back in their salon at the Bellagio, James got right back to work, as usual.

"So now we have our final question. Sex." James sat at the ready, pen and notepad in hand.

"What's the question?" Annie teased.

James chuckled. "The real question is: did you have any sexual escapades that readers would be interested in? Famous people? Shocking practices? Anything kinky, but not so kinky as to lose our soft porn customers."

"Nobody can beat Betty's story. Whew. Top of the heap there." Dolly shook her head in wonder. "The biggest muckety-muck possible."

"Yes, that's true. But this isn't a competition. Just tell me about anybody readers might care about," James instructed.

"My sex life would put your readers to sleep. It's real snooze material," Ginger admitted. "Nobody famous or even interesting. I had a typical high school boyfriend, a number of lovers when I was dancing, a brief affair with Balls Been-a-dick, that one disastrous marriage – now, he probably has some good sex stories that don't include me, the bastard – and since then I've dated maybe three guys long enough to have hit the rack with them. None of them lasted. There was one I really liked, and he claimed to be in love with me, but then I found out he was married. I kicked his ass to the curb. I sort of hate men. Except you, of course."

"I'm glad to hear you're not throwing me into the same category as those scoundrels," James said. "I promise there are more men out here who deserve not to be hated."

"Oh, I know, I know. I just need to get better at finding them. My friends here keep telling me for that to happen I need to leave my apartment more often and meet more people. I know that's true."

"Good advice. I hope you do that. Okay ..." James looked around "... who's next?"

"Me. Me." Annie fluffed her hair and did a little bounce on her behind. Dolly had noticed that the woman liked to do that bounce when she was excited about something. This should be good, she thought. Annie continued with, "Well, as everyone here likes to scold me about, yes, I worked as a Lady of the Night when I was dancing."

"Ah, Annie," Ginger interrupted, "I do believe you were a Lady of Anytime Night or Day."

Nonplussed, Annie continued. "True. And I made a fortune at it. There were a number of politicians, but nobody really big like Betty, damn it. I would've loved to snag one of those. But these gentlemen were mostly local and state politicians. I don't even remember their names. I'm not sure I ever knew their names."

"Did you ever see them on the news?" James wanted to know. "Were they big enough for that?"

"No. But that doesn't mean anything. I've never watched the news. I mean, what does it have to do with me? Anyway, one of them, I remember, was a Lieutenant Governor somewhere, one of the 'A' states. But I don't remember which one."

"'A'?"

"Yeah, you know, like Arkansas or Alabama. What's that other one?"

"Arizona?" Dolly suggested.

"Maybe Alaska?" Merry offered.

"No, I would've felt cold if it was Alaska. I don't know where it was. Aruba? Is that a state?" Heads shook all around. "Oh, I don't know. Anyway, he's probably the biggest politician I ever knew. Then there were singers and band members in our shows."

"And Balls," Ginger reminded her.

"Yeah, him, too, but he hardly counted. He wasn't that great. My real sex life began when I married Pookie. He was already 70 but, my god, he had a voracious sex drive. Five times a day sometimes at first. There were times it got in the way of my shopping and stuff. I don't even know how many times I was late for a hair appointment or massage or facial because he grabbed me when I was going out the door. He liked doing some things I'd never heard of but nothing too kinky. No threesomes or anything. But scary stuff. He was a real thrill seeker. A dare-devil."

"Oh, really." James' interest peaked. "Scary how?"

"Well, there was the time he wanted to try to do it on a trapeze."

"What?" Dolly gasped. "A trapeze like way up in the air?"

"Sure. What other kind is there? I'm scared of heights, but he insisted that would help me get over my fear. There's a name for that, but I don't remember what it is."

"Acrophobia," James said.

"Yeah. That. So we went to this circus training camp in Florida for a week. He rented a whole circus tent and hired a trainer, a real trapeze artist. Of course, he didn't know anything about Pookie wanting to have sex with me up there." She pointed upward. "I was terrified, but eventually learned to swing. I fell into the net a lot, though. Then when we got good enough, Pookie told the trainer to go away and had his bodyguards stand outside so nobody would come in. We stood together on the platform while he held the swing, then he sat down on it facing me while he held onto the platform bar, then I sat on his lap facing him. Do you see what I mean? His legs were on one side and mine went around his hips and were on the other side of the trapeze."

James closed the gape of his mouth. "Yeah, I get it." His voice sounded hoarse. He took a sip of his water.

"He had his fly open and I was naked under my little trapeze dress. He already had a boner by the time I got into place. Then he let go of the bar and we went swinging. There we are swinging back and forth, and he's pumping at the same time. It was quite a thrill."

"I can only imagine." James cleared his froggy throat.

"How did it end?" Dolly inquired, curious as hell.

"Oh, I fell off and he screamed because that sort of, you know, bent his poor pecker when I tumbled backwards. But he was okay. Then he jumped into the net, too, and we finished there."

"Wow. I've never heard of such a thing." Merry was floored.

"I didn't know such a thing was even possible," Layla added in astonishment.

"Yeah, there's only one thing wrong with that scenario," Ginger harped. "I don't believe a word of it."

"It doesn't matter what you believe." Annie took a sip of her wine. "If you don't believe that one, you'll never believe what we did next."

"I'm sure I won't." Ginger would not give it up.

Annie ignored her antagonist and barreled ahead. "Once he wanted to see if we could do it skydiving. You know how two people can be strapped together and jump with one person's back to the other person's front. Guess who was behind me." She giggled. "He had our jumpsuits specially made so we could do it."

"If you're afraid of heights, wasn't that terrifying for you?" James asked. "That would be a lot worse than a trapeze. So much higher. Had you jumped before?"

"Nope. Never. And, yes, I was terrified. But Pookie kept reassuring me that he would take care of me. I trusted him, and it worked out like he said. Sort of. I did kind of pass out when we first jumped, and it never did work out to have sex in the air. But we finished on the ground before the guys who came to get us could get there. It was fine."

Annie finished her story and no one spoke until Dolly said, "Annie, it sounds almost as if he talked you into doing things that scared you. Wasn't that a bit abusive?"

"Pfft. No. I wanted to please him."

Patiently, sweetly, as was her style, Merry said, "Annie, did you feel like you had to do those scary things to keep him happy in your marriage?"

Annie looked stricken, as if she'd never considered that before. "Maybe. I don't know. But I did it and I'm not sorry. In return, I got all the perks of a fabulously rich lifestyle. That is until my flaming asshole stepson took it all back." She guzzled the rest of her wine.

"Well, they might feel a little sorry for you because you say you had to do scary things," Ginger proffered, "but I'm still not buying a word of it. First you say you come from a wealthy family in Palm Springs, Florida, and none of them minded that you were a hooker and panty peeler. Then you claim you liked that work. Now you claim you and your 'pookie'..." Ginger rolled her eyes "... had a great sex life, you did dangerous things, and you liked that, too. I think you're full of shit."

Dolly scooched to the edge of the sofa, ready to intervene if another scuffle broke out, because Annie didn't ignore Ginger this time.

"Okay," Annie said, her voice wild and raw as she glared at Ginger, "my real name is Ansa Frydenlund. I come from a piss-poor, fanatically religious, strict farm family in Minnesota. I hated them as much as they hated me. They kicked me out when I was 15. I had to make my own way in this life, and I did. My 'pookie' and I did have an okay but boring sex life until he got too old. I haven't had sex in years. There. Do you like that better?"

Ginger considered the question. "I think that last part about your husband is possibly true. The rest, I have no idea. It's impossible to tell if you're ever telling the truth."

"What does it matter? Nobody cares what the truth is. They just like stories. Did you write all that down, James? Tell both stories and let readers wonder which one is true."

"I'm wondering," James said.

"You'll never know, will you?" Annie got up and tromped to the kitchen to pour herself more wine.

Everyone watched her go. Dolly thought the woman was such an enigma, there truly was no way of ever knowing if anything that came out of her mouth was true.

"I guess we may as well move on." James looked at Merry and Layla.

"I'll go next," Merry offered, "because my story is short. You know about my affair with the priest."

"Yeah," Ginger interjected, "he was no saint and you were no Virgin Mary." She guffawed as Merry swatted her arm.

"Anyway, after that, I had a few boyfriends that were totally unexciting. When my daughter was 17, I fell in love with a doctor. But he had a passion for working with underserved populations and eventually moved to Central America. He asked me to come with him, but I didn't want to be so far away from my daughter, even though she was starting college. I honestly figured he'd come back someday and we'd be together. Three years later he married a beautiful young woman from Ecuador. Since then, I've dated some, with very little sex. Nothing marriage worthy. No one famous has ever asked me out. The end."

"Have you ever heard from the doctor again?" James asked.

"Only as friends for a couple of years after he got married. His mother still lived in Denver, so he came back to see her every year. He'd call to see how my daughter and I were doing. But that didn't last. We didn't have anything to say anymore."

Layla said, "My story is similar, in that it's short. I already told you about being so busy with the kids after my husband died, dating was the last thing on my mind. I never expected to find love so late in life ..." she fondled her engagement ring "... but it is sheer joy. I feel supremely blessed."

James jotted down notes and turned to Dolly. "What about you? You've already mentioned a couple of famous men. Sex, sort of, with the famous comedian Wolff Garstonn. A short marriage to the famous basketball player Rooster Farmer. A kiss from a yet-to-be dictator Fidel Castro. Anybody else?"

"Not really. Nobody else famous besides some musicians and singers who became famous after we dated. But I don't want to talk about that. I want to talk about the best sex of my life. He may not have been famous, but he was the best lover any woman could ever have because he knew how to love."

"Oh, do tell," Annie spurred Dolly on as she came back and sat amongst them again, refilled wine glass in hand.

"I know who it is." Merry smiled.

"Me, too," Ginger said.

"I can guess," Layla added.

"Well then, do tell," James encouraged.

Dolly smiled and began the story of the best sex of her life.

"Me, too," Ginger said.

"I can guess," Layla added.

"Well then, do tell," James encouraged.

CHAPTER 17

"I'm not saying that sex at any particular age is better than sex at another age. It's just different at different stages of our lives. As long as the partners care about one another, both consent to what they're doing, and nobody gets hurt, it's all good."

"I'll drink to that." Annie gulped her wine.

"I agree." Ginger sighed. "And I haven't had nearly enough of it in a long time."

Merry chimed in. "I sure have enjoyed what I've had."

"I must say," Layla said, "later-in-life sex is amazing. I recommend it to everyone."

Dolly nodded agreement. "I've thought a lot about why having sex with my husband Otis was so good and have come to the conclusion there are a number of reasons. It wasn't that we were physically beautiful like when we were young, although I believe we were physically beautiful in a new way. And it wasn't because we still had raging hormones. It was because we cared about each other so deeply. I don't think most of us as young adults were even capable of that kind of caring. I know I certainly wasn't. I was far too self-absorbed and cock-eyed sure of myself. There's nothing wrong with being self-assured – in fact that's great – but self-absorbed is different.

"I didn't know how to compromise and come to a ..." She thought for a moment to come up with the right word. "I didn't know how to come to a consensus. Not in terms of giving up on my hopes and dreams but coming to an understanding on a more intimate level. Once in a while watching a movie with your partner because he asked you to, even if it isn't your favorite kind of movie. And he does the same with you. Once in a while making the chicken casserole without rice that you like but he doesn't. And sometimes he eats it with rice because you made it. And once in a while adjusting your schedule to spend more time with him if he asks you to. And he goes out of his way to make time for you, too. Things like that.

"Oh, I suppose some people know all of that right out of the womb. But I was a late bloomer. Okay, I admit, I was a late, late, late bloomer. I let my need to dance completely dominate my life. Interestingly, nobody ever asked me to give that up. They just asked that I make time for them, too. I'm not saying I regret anything I've ever done. I've made a conscious decision not to have regrets. Instead, I like to think of it as having learned along the way. By the time I married Otis, I had finally learned to share my life.

"So ... back to the sex. We were both 53 when we got married, so we were still pretty spry. I had finally learned to use sex toys, so we both enjoyed that. We had a blast shopping at Champs stores for toys and would giggle like teenagers over all the stuff in there."

"I'm sure Charlie would want to thank you for your patronage," James said.

"We went to Champs theaters, too, and loved so many of those movies, like I said before. Soft porn, a lot of which I now know you wrote." She nodded at James. He returned the nod.

"We were married for fifteen years," she continued, "and as we grew older sex became less spontaneous and more intentional. We often talked about how it almost became like being a high school kid again, where you flirt a lot but don't have a chance to have sex a lot. Otis and I flirted outrageously. It was so much fun. The best part was not feeling like that had to lead to having sex. It could simply lead to more fun teasing and touching. I loved that so much."

"Ah, I think our readers will like this part about the flirting," James noted. "Tell us more."

Dolly considered the question before answering. "It was little things. The way he would always open a door for me and gently put his hand in the middle of my back when we walked into a restaurant. He always waited for me to order first. He never started the car until I was buckled in. We would pass each other in the kitchen and softly touch an arm or back. We hugged every day and when one of us left the house, we both always said, 'I love you.' We paid attention and looked into the other person's eyes when they were talking.

"But we didn't smother each other or anything. We both still worked for the first half of our marriage. We belonged to a bowling league together, but we had separate hobbies, too. He played poker every week with his friends and played golf in the summertime. I enjoyed doing charity work with my church. And I had lunch with some of my church lady friends on a regular basis. We had busy lives."

An unconscious grin struck as she reflected. "We usually had music playing. A good song would come on and he'd take my hand and we'd dance in the middle of the living room, or kitchen, or wherever we were. R&B, boogie-woogie, swing, bebop, ballroom, soul. You name it, we liked it. I'd never paid any attention to country music until I met Otis. He was a big fan. Hank Williams Jr., Reba McIntire, George Strait. Charley Pride and Alabama. The list goes on and on. Otis taught me country-western dancing and we had so much fun at a country-western club. But I think I danced more in our own house than I ever did on stage. I'd always favored soul, so Aretha could sing anything, and we'd dance to it. *Respect* always got us going. And Patti LaBelle's *Lady Marmalade*." She chuckled. "Remember that one?"

"Sure." Layla pushed on her cane to stand up and swayed her hips and sang. "Hey sista, go sista, soul sista...."

Annie hopped up to make it a duet. Ginger and Merry followed for a quartet.

"Well, what the hell." Dolly couldn't resist. She got up to join in as the quintet pulled off a somewhat on-key rendition of the high-spirited song.

It ended up being a sort of sloppy chorus girl routine as they tried to stay in step with one another. When they got to the chorus, "Gitchi, gitchi, ya-ya, da-da ..." they ramped it up. Finished, they fell onto the couch in laughter as James applauded.

"I always wondered what that meant," James said. "Gitchi, gitchi, ya-ya, da-da."

"It can mean whatever you want," Annie giggled as she slapped his knee.

"Man, I loved *Respect*, too. Hey! That could be our Burly-Q Girl theme song. It's perfect for us. We never got enough respect as performers." Ginger glowed with enthusiasm over her own idea.

"That's right," Merry agreed.

"Yeah. Let's try it." Layla pushed herself up once more and started it off.

The others joined her again, and this time their song-and-dance routine came off more professionally, but it still left them in a fit of laughter when they were done.

"Whew." Dolly fanned herself. "That was fun."

Everyone plopped back down onto the couch.

"We have a theme song!" Annie cheered as she clapped.

"Hey, that gives me an idea," Ginger chirped. "I can give us all matching tattoos. Something simple here." She drew her idea onto her upper arm with her finger. "'Burly-Q Girls' in a heart or something."

"How about with a heart-shaped pastie and tassel?" Dolly suggested, picturing it as she talked.

"Yes!"

"I want one!"

"Me, too!"

"James, would you like one, too, to commemorate your work with this unruly gang?" Dolly teased as he shook his head.

"I'll pass on that. It's a girl thing. But thanks, anyway. Now, I'm not entirely sure how our conversation about sex went completely off the rails and ended up with all of that, but I'm glad it did."

"Oh, yeah. Sex. Well, Otis and I did flirt a lot, but we also enjoyed making love. One of our favorite songs was *Bring It on Home to Me*. There's just something about that song that usually landed us in the bedroom."

"Uh huh," Layla moaned. "Sam Cooke's voice could do that to a girl."

"Oh yeah," Merry groaned.

"I'd never kick him outta bed for eating crackers," Ginger lamented.

"Sweet lovin'," Annie sighed.

Dolly's face softened at the memory.

DETROIT, 1987

· · ·

"Miss O'Dare, may I have the honor of this dance?"

Dolly looked up from the chicken cacciatore recipe she'd been studying in a cookbook at the kitchen table.

Otis held out his hand. Sam Cooke sang *Bring It on Home to Me* from the record player in the living room, and she got a kick out of the obvious setup.

"Why yes, sir, I believe you may." She placed her hand in his and the warmth of him radiated from his fingertips up to the top of her head and down to the tips of her toes. She stood up and melted into his arms.

Otis was a fabulous dancer. Moving to music while enmeshed in his body felt like floating on heaven's own cloud. Holding her right hand out in a proper dance stance, his other hand started out around her waist. But it inched its way up her back to ignite her spine and set her body on fire.

She nestled her cheek into his neck and inhaled the scent of his tantalizing Old Spice. When she kissed that neck, he groaned with pleasure.

"You know, Miss O'Dare, I've been thinking – now, I don't want to be too forward or anything – but I've been thinking that perhaps we could hit the rack."

"Oh, really? My, you are rather forward, aren't you?"

"Yes, I am. How can I help it with you in my arms?"

"Hit the rack, as in that bed right in there?" She taunted him, pointing at their bedroom.

"Yes, that very one."

She slipped out of his embrace, led him by the hand to the bedroom door, and looked inside, feigning innocence. "You mean this bed that we could so easily fall into right now if we wanted to?"

"I do."

"But weren't you getting ready to go to poker night with the guys? I mean, you'll miss a hand or two …"

Her sultry delivery worked, according to what emerged to greet her as she unzipped his jeans.

"That's okay because I'm thinking the odds are better here," he said gamesomely. "You're a sure bet."

He kissed her hair as she fondled his erection.

"Oh really? You're that sure of yourself?"

"I am, because I've been the luckiest man alive since the day I first laid eyes on you."

That did it. That and the crooning in the background to "bring it on home to me" fanned the flames of her desire into wildfire.

Dolly knelt down on her knees and took him into her mouth. After a few strokes, she raised her head and said, "This looks like a full house to me."

"Oh, baby, you have no idea. It's a royal flush, as good as it gets."

She cooed and went back to her pursuit until he invited her to get into bed with him, where he stacked the deck and brought it on home.

LAS VEGAS, 1995

RELUCTANTLY, Dolly pulled herself out of her memory of hot sex and forced herself to come back to the cold reality of the air-conditioned salon. She sighed. Her audience sat there staring at her, mum.

"What else do you want to know?" she asked.

Her girlfriends let loose and took turns gushing over how touched they were by her story.

"I agree," James offered. "It's refreshing to hear about a husband-wife bond like that. It'll be good to have that kind of intimacy included in the book." He looked up at the ceiling in thought, then brought his eyes back to her. "What else might there have been that brought you two so close together?"

Again, Dolly paused while considering her response. Then she said, "I think it shows love that we took care of the boring stuff of life. We made sure the bills were paid and insurance was set and wills were updated in case anything happened to one of us and the other was left to handle everything alone. That might not sound lovey-dovey to some people, but I'm here to tell you it's the best. Caring about the other person, doing whatever you can to eliminate stress in their life, whether you're going to be there or not. That's love.

"In fact, when he got sick with prostate cancer and we found out it was too far along and he wouldn't be cured, he told me he hoped I'd find love again. I refused to hear of it, but he insisted I pay attention. He said I'd been alone too much of my life; he didn't want me to be alone again. He was totally selfless. I don't think I could ever be so selfless.

"But then one day something struck me, and I teased him about it: I said the only reason he didn't care if I got married again was because he knew he'd always be number one in my heart, no matter who else was number two. He laughed and said, 'Of course.'"

She paused again, forming her words for the rest of the story. She'd thought of these things many times but had never shared all these thoughts with anyone.

"We found out he had cancer when he was 67, one year before his death. We needed to start being careful because he was on some heavy-duty drugs. There could be side effects on his heart. I was more concerned about it than he was, but he finally convinced me that if he was going to die from this thing, he wanted to enjoy our life together as much as possible before he went. I had to accept his wish. It was his life. I needed to let go and allow him to live it as he pleased. But, of course, I didn't always do a good job of that. When we had sex, though, it became more precious than ever, even more meaningful than before. It's impossible to put into words how deep our bond became. Impending death will do that to a couple."

Dolly stopped talking then, and James didn't try to goad her into saying any more. She figured he had everything he needed for the book. She certainly had said everything she needed to say.

CHAPTER 18

"*L*adies." The Elvis impersonator, Rhett, rushed over to the Burly-Q Girls, who stood backstage in the theater at the Flamingo where they'd been serving as support team for Malika while she prepared for her performance. "We have front row seats for you. Your writer friend James has already been seated there. Follow me."

One by one they hugged Malika and wished her well, then followed Rhett, who wore his full Elvis regalia but had forgone an Elvis speech pattern when talking to them. The Elvis sound was fun, but Dolly loved his natural mellow voice. He led them down some sidesteps, taking Layla's arm to help her, and ushered them to the front row, where James awaited them.

They piled in with Dolly first, so she ended up sitting next to their "writer friend". They'd already had a spectacular evening with James treating them to dinner at the toney Lago Italian restaurant at the Bellagio, where they sat overlooking the fountains. He'd given each of them an envelope with a $1,000 check and a gift box from Tiffany's, compliments of Charlie Champ he said, although Dolly wondered if he'd done it himself. Each of them received a gold bracelet with a red pave heart-shaped bangle with a diamond in the center.

Dolly's crush on James swelled to near bursting. He truly was a good guy.

She felt proud of what they'd all accomplished together. She also felt glamorous for the first time since memory served. They all had dressed up for the evening, and she knew that she and her friends looked stunning. All heads had turned to ogle them as they trouped into the restaurant. The show-woman in her, she discovered, still lived. Thanks to Annie and their infamous shopping spree, she, Ginger, and Merry had purchased "party clothes", among so many other things, without really knowing why except that it was fun to have them. Now they were glad to put them to good use.

Dolly adored her black dress infused with silver sparkles that accentuated her silver hair. Its lowcut front displayed her cleavage, too. She'd loaned a fancy red dress to Betty – thankfully they were the same size – and the Corn Pone Queen looked great, with her tiara in her overdyed beehive somehow seeming just right. Ginger wore a green number that brought out her beautiful green eyes and green-framed glasses and highlighted her bright red hair. Merry wore a slinky white garment that made her look like a Roman goddess, with her white hair piled high atop her head. Layla had on a leopard print dress that perfectly complimented her exotic beauty and her gray-streaked dark hair. Annie outdid them all, of course, in a strapless gold lamé cocktail dress that matched her showy dyed blond hair. She'd accessorized with new diamond jewelry. Dolly wore her diamond stud earrings and was pleased to have them after wondering if she'd ever actually wear the honkers again.

The lights in the theater went down. Silence filled the cavernous room. The emcee, a man in a black tuxedo looking very much like he impersonated a butler, came onstage carrying a microphone. A spotlight hit him.

"Ladies and gentlemen, we are delighted to bring you a surprise this evening. A performer we met only a couple of days ago has graced us with her presence and agreed to perform for us. Believe me, folks, this might be a conference for impersonators, but this is no imposter. She's the real deal. I bring you Malika!"

The audience applauded politely, not knowing what this might bring. The spotlight went off and the emcee walked off stage as muted lights went up on stage. Traditional Middle Eastern music began to play from a sound system. Malika appeared, slowly undulating her way to center stage. A communal gasp went up from the audience in appreciation of her beauty. She wore a costume that had been made and worn by her grandmother, the one Dolly remembered, with a gold-coin-encrusted bra top and a matching wide belt, and a diaphanous floor-length skirt with a slit up one leg. Malika masterfully unwrapped a filmy veil that had covered her captivating face and bewitching body and fluttered it through the air in rhythm to the music. To Dolly, and to the others too, she guessed, Malika looked exactly like her grandmother had looked on stage.

Dolly leaned forward to glance at Layla. The woman's worshipping gaze was affixed to her granddaughter as if the young woman was holy. Of course, to Layla she was.

Dolly could see that Superman had appeared, and he and Elvis sat at the end of the row. She wished she sat closer to suggest they close their gaping mouths.

She sat back and watched as the young woman performed like an ethereal, transcendent star. The music had started out slow and sultry, with Malika appearing to be lost in a dreamlike state for many tantalizing long minutes. The audience sat spellbound, lost in the dream with her. When the music picked up the pace, Malika began the hip thrusts, figure eights, and belly rolls that were common in belly dancing. But when she did them, they took on new life. Her perfectly molded body, large breasts, chiseled features, and toned arms and legs moved effortlessly to the call of the tune. Her mastery of belly rolls – from the top down, from the bottom up, and in the center – had left her with an abdomen like a comic book female superhero. A sheen appeared on Malika's velvety skin, a nod to the effort she put forth for her audience.

When she dropped to her knees for floor work and threw her veil into the air at the same moment she executed a backbend, the audience gasped when the veil floated down through the air and landed across her face and hair. On her knees with her back arched until the crown on her head touched the floor behind her, she didn't use her hands or arms for support. Instead, her arms floated out at her sides with delicate handwork. The audience sat rapt, all eyes glued to the astounding spectacle before them. Pumping her body up and down in a teasing display as she remained in the backbend, her long hair would splay out on the floor, then rise until the tips barely touched the floor, then lower again. Finally, she slid her hands underneath the veil and lifted it off her face with her hands in prayer position, like a woman freeing herself from any sins of the soul. The music worked its way into a frenzy as she grabbed the veil, rolled onto her side to sit up, and reached out to the audience with the veil flowing from her hand, as if beckoning them to love her. Quickly, she stood up and pranced around the stage shimmying her breasts and hips in a display of utter joy to be alive. Suddenly, after a thunderous strike of the doumbek drum, the music stopped. Malika froze. Solemnly gazing out at her audience, she then smiled so radiantly it seemed as if the entire crowd returned the favor. The music started up again and Malika gaily swished her way off stage.

Applause and cheering filled the room as they gave a standing ovation. Not to be outdone, Superman and Elvis both hooted, hollered, whistled, and clapped riotously. Dolly joined in the fun and let go with a round of "bravo", which made James laugh.

Satisfied and slap happy, they started to leave when Superman and Elvis stopped them as they exited their row. "Come with us, please," Elvis said.

They were led back up the sidesteps and behind the stage. Elvis and Superman each took one of Layla's arms and lifted her up the steps.

"Oh, Malika wants to see us," Layla gushed.

But Malika was nowhere in sight.

The emcee was back onstage saying something they couldn't quite catch as people appeared out of nowhere to thrust props at them. Roy Rogers gave Ginger his cowboy hat, fringed vest, and cap gun. Merry got Betty Crocker's frilly apron. Annie was given an enormous feather fan by Sally Rand, but this one in a flesh-colored body tight rather than naked like the real-life stripper. Marilyn Monroe gave Dolly a pair of satiny above-the-elbow opera gloves. Betty got a pink feather boa from Marlene Dietrich. And Malika appeared and tied her veil around her grandmother's waist.

"What's this?" Layla asked, although the others had figured it out.

"You're going onstage, Grandma," Malika announced. "Give it all you've got."

"But, but ..." Layla stammered. "I can't." She held up her cane.

"I have all the faith in the world that you can." Malika kissed Layla on the cheek. "Okay, girls, go have fun!" she said to them all as she motioned for them to get onstage.

Annie didn't waste one second. She trounced onstage fluttering her fan before anyone else could blink.

"Ah!" The emcee said. "This must be Annie Fannie!"

Ginger bounced on next, twirling her cap gun and then shooting at random.

"And here we have Ginger Snapper!"

Merry went on, coquettishly throwing kisses.

"This must be Sister Merry!"

Dolly sashayed on, playfully pulling down one glove as if considering stripping.

"And Dolly O'Dare!"

Betty walked on looking like a deer in the headlights but quickly acclimated and twirled the end of her boa.

"I'm afraid I don't know you, miss," the emcee admitted.

Betty snatched his mic, looked deadpan at the audience, and declared, "I'm Betty, the Arkansas Corn Pone Queen of 1960 and 3."

Layla came on last, slowly walking with her trusty cane. She picked up the edge of the veil and waved with it in her hand.

"And this," the emcee said, "is Lovely Layla, Malika's grandmother, the woman who taught her granddaughter to belly dance like you just witnessed!

The audience had clapped for each woman as she came on stage. And they'd laughed and clapped adoringly at Betty. But they gave Layla the same kind of standing ovation Malika had received.

"Here they are, ladies and gentlemen! The Flamingo Hotel presents the Burly-Q Girls!" The emcee dramatically swept his arm toward them as he walked off stage.

Aretha Franklin singing "Respect" boomed from the sound system. Malika had obviously spilled the beans about their theme song. The women all looked at one other and the unspoken message resounded across the stage. They were performers at heart and were never going to get a chance to do this again, so they may as well make it good.

And that they did.

They strutted, wiggled, shimmied, and teased. At one point Dolly looked over to see Layla standing firmly on both feet with her cane balanced on her head, much like she'd done back in the day, except then she could walk and hip thrust without ever losing the cane. Annie was having the time of her life, and Ginger had no problem pretending to shoot people, occasionally aiming at Annie. Merry fluttered her ruffled apron at the crowd, and Betty surprised everyone by hamming it up with the best of them. She really had missed her calling, Dolly thought.

The crowd did not disappoint. Dolly realized how much she'd missed applause and this room full of impersonators, kindred spirits that they were, fed her longing. She soaked in the accolades and felt her heart swell with delight.

As the song ended and they took a bow; however, somebody in the back of the room hollered, disrupting the finale of their show. A grumble went through the crowd at the disturbance, but then the intruder shrieked loudly enough to be heard onstage.

"It's Balls!"

Everyone in the room had known that the Burly-Q Girls wanted to get their hands on one Ballard Benedict, so everyone turned around to see if the man himself actually had enough balls to show his face here. Sure enough, there he was in the back of the theater standing at the door, seeming confused as to why he'd garnered so much attention.

Dolly shoved everyone out of the way, flew down the steps off the stage, and jolted down the aisle. Merry, younger and in better shape, passed her. Ginger and Annie weren't far behind. Before it could dawn on Balls what was going on so he could make a clean getaway, Popeye's Olive Oil came out of nowhere and made a dive for his knees. He went down like a felled tree. Merry and half a dozen more impersonators – Elvis, Superman, Betty Crocker, Spock, Batman, and Madonna – piled on. Dolly, breathless, caught up in time to see Balls curled into a protective fetal ball on the floor, his arms wrapped around his head like a turtle gone into its shell.

He cried out in terror. "Wait! Wait! You have the wrong man. I don't know what this is about, but it wasn't me!" He dared to look around, only to spy four clients encroaching upon him with an angry horde behind them. He looked from Dolly to Merry to Ginger to Annie. "Oh, hi, girls." He threw them a little wave. "My, you look lovely. Long time no see," he muttered obsequiously, reality sinking in.

Now he knew what this was all about and knew he was the right man, after all.

<h1 style="text-align:center">CHAPTER 19</h1>

"Wait. Let me get this straight." Dolly squinted malevolently at the little man. "You claim you didn't steal our money, but your 'fiancé' did?"

"That's correct. Former fiancé. Don't forget that part."

They sat in Elvis' room, which he'd generously donated for the cause. Balls had been dragged up there by the men and then the women asked that the room be cleared so they could conduct an interrogation. They knew that a curious and protective crowd remained gathered outside the door.

"I've had a really rough time," Balls lamented like a prisoner on death row.

"Oh, boo-fucking-hoo," Ginger spat. "I don't believe one fucking word you say."

A knock came at the door, and Merry opened it a slit. It was Layla, having caught up with them.

She came in and said, "I had so many nice people offer to help me. The Hulk picked me right up in his arms and carried me all the way here." She leaned in on her cane and glared at their suspect. "So, here we are with our infamous Balls Been-a-dick."

181

"Youse guys call me that? I'm crushed." He put a fist to his concave chest, feigning being crushed.

Dolly thought him quite pathetic. He seemed decidedly shorter than she remembered. His hair was brown at the tips but had missed many a dye job and was mostly gray. At least what was left of it. His balding crown gleamed like a bowling ball. He looked and smelled like a homeless man, and now they knew he was indeed the decrepit old man they'd sought out and missed at that shoddy motel a couple of days earlier.

Another knock came at the door and Ginger answered to be handed their purses, which they'd left at their seats. She thanked the deliverer and turned back to the room with a wicked gleam in her eye.

"Here it is," she announced with pleasure. Tossing the other purses aside, she opened hers and pulled out her tattoo wand, holding it up for all to see.

"What's that?" Balls became nervous, sweat breaking out on his brow. "What ya gonna do with that?"

"You'll see," Ginger said in a sing-song voice as she plugged it in. "Girls, grab him."

With two women holding down each arm – Layla sat in the only armchair and watched – Ginger unceremoniously unzipped Balls' pants and pulled out his penis.

He yelped and squirmed with all his might.

Ginger sniggered.

"What you doin' with that thing?" His eyes became as big as saucers as his eyes glommed onto the wand as it heated up. "Wait. You know that thing is awful old."

"You talking about this?" Ginger held up the wand. "Or this?" She flicked his pecker with her finger.

"Owww!"

"Don't worry about this. It's the old kind but it works well enough for what we have planned for you. A tattoo of a big, ugly, open wound, so no woman will ever want to touch your wiener again."

"Unless," Dolly interjected, "you tell us where our money is at and tell us how we can get it back. Now. If you've spent it all and it's gone, then tough luck for you."

"I told you. That bitch I thought I was engaged to took it all. I'm dead broke. Look at me." He shrugged and looked down at his withered body. "That's obvious. I'd give you every cent if I could."

Ginger grabbed his penis and headed for the kill.

Balls hollered and writhed, but his captors held on tight to his arms.

The hot tip of the tattoo wand was about to hit its mark when Balls cried out. "Nobody touches my schlong anymore anyway. I mean, look at me. Who would want me?"

Ginger paused. Everyone stared at his withered-up schlong. He certainly did seem to make sense.

"Ginger, don't you dare fall for that," Annie insisted as she held his arm in a hold like a vice.

Ginger looked at her, confused.

"Oh, shit. Here, give it to me," Annie snarled as she wrenched the hot wand out of Ginger's hand. She had no problem going in for the kill, grabbing Balls' penis and tattooing a squiggly line onto it.

He screamed in pain.

Every other woman in the room went for the wand to stop her. In the tussle, the hot instrument thrashed about in Anne's hand. Balls ducked this way and that, like a boxer, to avoid being struck in the face and having another unwelcome tattoo, this one evident to the world. Finally, Ginger snatched the wand.

"Oh my god. Oh my god. Oh my god," Balls whimpered, his hands on his chest now that his arms were free. He struggled to breathe. Quickly, with shaking hands, he repacked his pecker, zipped up his pants, and held both hands over himself like a protective athletic cup. He moaned in simmering pain.

Another knock came at the door. "Everything okay in there?" James hollered.

"Yes, James. No problem. We're fine," Dolly yelled back.

"Okay, let's all calm down," Merry advised. "Balls, take some deep breaths." She went to the mini fridge, pulled out a bottle of water, and opened it. "Here, drink this." She handed it over.

He guzzled mightily, then seemed a bit revived.

Ginger still held the wand as if contemplating what to do with it. Dolly advised her to unplug it and take it into the bathroom to set on the granite countertop while it cooled down. Ginger did so, and by the time she came back everyone seemed to have gathered their wits about them.

Except Annie. "You son-of-a-bitch," she hurled at their foe. "If your 'fiancé' stole our money, how in God's name did you let that happen?"

"Well, it's a long story."

"Make it short and simple," Dolly insisted.

"Well, you see, I sorta went through a midlife crisis, kinda later, though."

"We know," Dolly said. "We watched it happen. We didn't see you or talk to you often, but when we did we could tell you'd gone over the edge."

"Yeah," Ginger affirmed. "I'd see you around town every now and then or stop at your office, and you'd clearly gone bat-shit crazy."

"Looney Tunes," Merry added.

"Bonkers," Annie offered.

"Berserk," Layla interjected.

"Sounds to me like you need to be cutting out paper dolls in the looney bin," Betty said.

They'd found places to sit on the edge of the bed and on the arm of Layla's chair, with Merry taking the floor and Annie pacing.

"I can't believe you're going to let this bastard get away with this," Annie spewed. "You're wusses, all of you." She gestured wildly.

"Annie, let it rest," Dolly cajoled. "Here, come sit by me." Dolly patted the spot on the bed beside her.

Annie huffed, plastered on her pout, sat down, and crossed her legs, pumping her top leg furiously.

"Now," Dolly went on, "back to your late midlife crisis." She pointed at Balls.

"Well, youse guys wouldn't understand the pressure it is for a guy like me to get old. I mean in this business. When your clients all start to retire, you're caput. So I had to try to look younger to attract younger clients. Ya know what I mean? Not that I hadn't already made a fortune, 'cuz I had. But I wouldn't know what to do with myself if I didn't stay in the game. Ya know? Anyways, I guess I start thinking I really am younger, and I find me a pretty, young accountant. My old one kicked the bucket. I mean, there's a good one right next door to my office. But do I stop to consider it might be smart to go with him? No-o-o. I fall for a broad."

"You were thinking with your dick." Annie hurled out the accusation.

"Well, yeah, Annie, sweetie, I guess I was."

"Don't call me 'sweetie', you flaming asshole."

"Okay, I didn't mean no offense. Anyways, like I said, she stole everything right out from under me."

"How was that possible?" Ginger seethed, having joined ranks with Annie in continuing to loathe their prey.

"Well, ya see, it starts after I buy her a Mercedes. We're in love, or at least that's what I think. So it's an engagement present. She already has a huge diamond engagement ring. But every time I go to see her at her apartment, the car is gone. She always says it's being washed. That's one damned clean car, I tell her. Then when I buy her a condo …"

"Wait. You bought her a condo when you didn't know what she'd done with the Mercedes?" Dolly was flabbergasted.

"Well, yeah. You know, dick thinking. Anyways, I make a surprise visit to the condo one day. Outside, I'm glad to see the Mercedes, so's I know she's home. I brought her flowers and stuff."

"Why weren't you living in the condo, too, if you bought it?" Merry wanted to know.

"Yeah. That's weird. Or why didn't she move in with you at your place?" Ginger asked.

"'Cuz she says she doesn't believe in livin' together 'til we're married."

"And, and you fell for that?" Annie sputtered.

"Sure." He pointed to his crotch. "She's planning a great big wedding and that's taking a long time. She wants to invite all her old stripper friends."

"She was your accountant, but she'd been a stripper," Dolly stated, putting the pieces together. "Okay. Go on."

"Yeah. Well, she's gonna move in with me after the wedding; then she'll sell the condo."

"You said 'she'll sell the condo.' Surely it wasn't in her name." Layla, the real estate agent that she was, was aghast.

"Sure. I mean, I was in love."

He started to point again but Dolly swatted his hand away. "Okay. We get it. Continue."

"So's I go there one day as a surprise, like I said, the car is parked outside, I'm all happy and tingly inside, I ring the bell, and a man answers the door. A tall stud in shorts and no shirt. Lots younger than yours truly. Muscles hanging out all over the place. I ask him who he is and what's he doing in my fiancé's apartment, and the bruiser laughs right in my face. She shows up behind him and gets real mad, yelling at me that I have no business coming to her place unannounced. She's hardly got any clothes on. So I surmise something hinky is goin' on here."

"No shit, Einstein," Ginger scoffed.

"Before I know what's happened, bruiser dude picks me right up off my feet and throws me to the curb. I hear her laughing as they slam the door. Well, now I know for sure I've been taken for a ride. She's living there with a boyfriend, and he ain't me."

Ginger opened her mouth to lob another snide remark, but Dolly threw her a look to hold it. Ginger snapped her mouth shut and shook her head in disbelief.

"I'm miserable, of course. My fiancé isn't really my fiancé and she has a boyfriend, so I go to a club and drink my sorrows away. It isn't until I sober up the next morning that I think about what she might have done to my business."

"No. Tell me you didn't give her access to all your accounts." Now Dolly was the one shaking her head.

"Well, sure. She was my accountant."

"So everything was gone, right?" Merry asked the question that would put the final nail in the coffin.

"Right. I didn't know it yet, but that's right. I went back to her condo the next day, real secret like, hiding at the end of the parking lot in my car, and she and the bozo are moving out. Then I checked the county records and she'd sold the place. Turns out she sold my place, too."

"How could she possibly have sold your condo, too?" Layla asked, incredulous.

"Well, ya see, I put my own condo in her name, too, along with my name, so even that was gone."

"Why was your condo in her name, too?" Dolly asked, having given up on being shocked.

"She wanted an early wedding gift."

Dolly sighed. "Of course she did."

They may as well have been sitting in a cemetery, the room

became so silent and gloomy. Eventually, Betty revived to come up with a question. "Did you report it to the police?"

"Not right away. I was embarrassed that I'd been such a sorry old sap. But after a few days, when I couldn't get a fix on where they'd gone, I reported it. The officer looked at me like I was the sorry old sap I knew I was. He said they'd look into it, but I know that some stupid old guy giving everything away to a former stripper is nothing new to them, and it ain't no priority. They don't care and will never look for them."

Now the room felt like a tomb, the death of their hopes of getting their money back closing in on them. No one knew what else to say.

Finally Ginger, unwilling to give the louse a break, broke the morose spell. "Hey, what about this thing we've figured out where you had affairs with me and Merry and Annie, and hit on Dolly, all at the same time? What was that all about, huh?" She stood up in front of him and shook a finger in his face.

"Oh, that. Surely you're not surprised. I mean, you were all so beautiful, how could I pick just one? You're all still beautiful, by the way." He attempted a wan smile.

The stares that elicited made Ballard Benedict – Balls Been-a-dick for sure – shrink in fear that the tattoo wand might come out again.

CHAPTER 20

Five Burly-Q Girls sat in the '50s Diner at one o'clock in the morning, looking a little worse for wear. Okay, a lot worse for wear. The remnants of their midnight breakfasts remained on the table until Betty couldn't take it anymore and hopped up to clear their plates. She had the night off, but the waitress on duty drove her nuts for being a "putz."

Annie was AWOL, which was why only five of them sat at the table. Silence had pressed in on the weary gang. They'd already agreed it'd been such a momentous night they'd have a hard time sleeping, so may as well stick together for a while longer. Champs Enterprises had extended their stay at the Bellagio for three more nights, so they could sleep all day tomorrow if they wanted.

Elvis sang "Are You Lonesome Tonight" from the jukebox, sending Dolly into a mood swing. So much had happened in one evening, she hardly knew what to think or feel.

James had left for the airport a couple of hours earlier, and she already missed him so much she felt glum. His leaving made her especially sad after they stole their first kiss out by the Bellagio fountains just before he went. She'd liked it. A lot. At least there was hope there. There didn't seem to be hope for getting their money back from Balls any time soon. But at least they now had the cash from the book to hire a private investigator, not to find Balls as they'd originally planned, but to find that fiancé con woman and her boyfriend accomplice.

Elvis got done being lonesome and "I Could Have Danced All Night" played. The mood around the table brightened.

"No matter what else has happened," Merry said, "being on stage again was fantastic."

"Oh my god, I loved it." Ginger swizzled her soda with its straw and took a long draw before adding, "I had no idea I missed it so much."

"I'd give anything if I could get out there and really shake it up again." Layla shook her head. "But watching my granddaughter is almost as good. I'm glad she loves it as much as I did."

"Yeah," Dolly said as her spirits lifted at the thought, "You did great, Layla. And I'll tell you what: Malika is you reincarnated on stage." There were nods all around. "We all did good. I loved it, too. I've always missed being on stage. Although, I wouldn't ever want to have to go through all that hard work again."

"Amen," Ginger said. "It was more hard work, at least to be good at it, than most people could ever imagine."

"I'm used to hard work." Betty gestured around the diner. "But I know this is nothing compared to performing. I wish I'd had enough guts to try it when I was younger. That made tonight especially wonderful for me. I can't thank y'all enough."

"Thank you," Dolly said. "You made our troupe complete. And I think we all know it's your story that's going to make our book sell."

Betty grunted. "I'm glad that tacky affair so long ago amounted to something worthwhile in my life."

Silence bore down again.

"It sure is quiet without Annie," Merry observed.

"We have to admit something," Dolly said. "Annie might be a total pain in the ass, but things are never boring when she's around."

"Yeah. I admit it. Does anybody know where she went?" Ginger asked.

"I don't know," Dolly said, "but that girl has been up to something all day. After last night you'd think she'd be pissed and depressed. But no. She was chipper all day. And now she's gone missing. There's no telling what she's …"

"Oh no." Ginger interrupted as she scrunched down in her seat, trying to disappear. "Look who's here."

"Hey! There you are. Hi, girls." Balls bounded into the room, pulled up a chair, and plopped himself down, uninvited.

"I thought you said you'd call us tomorrow to talk about finding that woman. What're you doing here?" Dolly asked indignantly.

"Now, now. Don't be upset. Let bygones be bygones. I mean, I lose your money, you prick my dick, we're all even. Right? I happened to be driving by and saw youse in here having a little family gathering without me."

"Family? You think you're part of our 'family'?" Ginger was insulted.

"Sure. It's like you're all sisters and I'm your brother or something."

"Brother? Good god, Balls, you slept with three of us," Dolly reminded him. "You are not our 'brother'."

"Okay then, how about cousin?"

"No." Merry held firm.

"Howse about adopted third cousin twice removed? Yeah, that'll work. Anyways, we're all in this mess together and I want to do whatever I can to get that money back. Not only for me, but for all a' youse, too. We hafta find that damned dame. So I'm thinking

191

youse all need to hire a dick. You know, the investigator kind. Not the other kind. Mine is doing fine, by the way."

"Nobody cares how yours is doing," Ginger snarled.

Something suddenly occurred to Dolly. She took a gander out the window and Balls' old Pinto sat in the middle of the small parking lot. "Balls, do you live in your car?"

"Sure. Where else would I live? Youse saw me get kicked outta my fancy motel."

The women looked at one another, their wordless communication code at work as they deciphered what to do. Dolly got the message that it was okay to go ahead and tell Balls they'd already planned on hiring a P.I. He was delighted.

"So's tomorrow we can get together and I'll tell you everything I know about ..." He stopped when everyone's attention was drawn to the door. He turned to look, too.

A tall, handsome man in a crisp, black chauffeur's uniform stood inside the door looking around, appearing as though he belonged on the cover of a romance novel. Spying them, he strode over; politely took off his hat to reveal thick, wavy hair; and said, "You must be the Burly-Q Girls. I have an invitation for you to join me for a private gathering at the Bellagio."

They sat there stunned. Ginger popped up out of her seat first. "Okay," she said enthusiastically.

"May I ask who's inviting us?" Dolly wanted to know even as she got up.

"It's a surprise," the hunk said. "I believe you'll be delighted."

"Wait a minute. Are you an impersonator from the convention and this is a joke?" Merry posited.

"I assure you, ma'am, I am no impersonator."

He was so serious, they were convinced. They filed out to the shiny black stretch limo parked in front of the diner. At the last second, Balls piled in with them.

Fifteen minutes later they were taking the private elevator up to the Bellagio penthouse and didn't know why. Ginger speculated that Annie had somehow hornswoggled her way back in and it would only be a matter of minutes before they got kicked out again. The other women didn't know what to think. Balls, though, had an opinion: his luck had finally changed and he was on his way "up." Nobody bothered to respond to that.

The familiar chime dinged as the elevator doors opened. No one moved. The scene in front of them was incomprehensible.

"Surprise!" Annie shouted as she waved a bouquet of white roses at them. Still in her gold lamé dress, a long white veil hung from the back of her hair. Most shockingly, Lemuel Jones – the heretofore loathed Junior, not the dearly departed Senior, of course – stood beaming at her side. "It's my wedding!" Annie shrieked gleefully. "Come in, come in, come in." She motioned them into the room.

They wobbled in like hypnotized zombies.

Dolly thought maybe she'd walked in on the filming of a horror flick, a real spookfest. *Bridezilla Meets Groomkilla*. A man who must be a preacher stood by the windows, Bible in hand. A white wedding cake sat on the dining table, which was covered in a delicate white lace tablecloth. Large vases filled with white roses were scattered about the room.

Wow, Dolly mused, what money can buy on a moment's notice.

Annie swept over to give each of them an exuberant kiss on the cheek, even Balls. Talk about letting bygones be bygones. The woman had gone way past bygones to bye-bye to the money he owed her.

"Okay," Annie said, her eyes bright with excitement and probably a flute or two or three of champagne, too, "I know you're wondering what's going on here. Well," she said as she wove her arm through her stepson's and pressed her body into his, "the minute I saw Pookie Junior here with his eyes glommed onto my boobs last night when we were practicing with our pasties …"

Balls nudged Dolly. "Youse goin' back onto the bus'ness?"

"Shut up, Balls."

"I knew right then and there," Annie went on, "that he liked me." She lifted a shoulder and covered her mouth with a hand, looking very much like a happy kid. The lovebirds kissed, and then Annie went on with her spiel. "So I called him this morning and invited him to meet me at the show tonight. I didn't know we'd be performing, but I thought we could have a drink or something. He says when he saw me on stage, he knew he had to propose."

Dolly wondered if "Pookie Junior" – did she really call him that? – ever actually said anything. She felt certain there had been a lot more conniving and plotting involved on Annie's part than a simple invitation to have a drink. So far this evening, Annie had done all the talking. As it turned out, they didn't hear the groom speak until he said "I do" during their vows.

After the ceremony, more invited guests came in, all looking uber rich and ultra stuffy. The girls gathered on the balcony, each with a plate of cake in hand and a flute of champagne in the other hand. Layla had to make two trips because of the need to use her cane. Once all gathered, they set down their glasses and dug into the cake.

Dolly had been juggling the bride's bouquet, which she'd tucked into the crook on her arm, and the cake and sparkly. Relieved of the bouquet and the glass, she took a big bite of her cake.

Merry pointed her fork at Dolly. "You have to admit, it was nice of Annie to give you the bouquet."

"Yeah, it's pretty obvious you and James have a crush on each other," Ginger teased in-between bites.

"I'd say the electricity in the room between you two was so red hot," Layla tittered, "we're lucky we didn't get singed in the process."

"I'm tellin' ya, girl; yer gonna be hitched agin 'fore long." Betty nodded confidently.

"Oh, don't be silly," Dolly scoffed. "I know James and I like each other, and he did invite me to dinner when I get back to Detroit. But I have long believed that after having three men in my life, I've had all any woman deserves."

"What do you mean, three?" Merry looked confused.

Ginger prodded Dolly's memory. "You had Bill and Otis."

"You've forgotten Rooster," Dolly reminded them.

"Oh, that bum. Rooster was a chicken-shit asshole." Ginger beamed at her analogy, especially when the others chuckled.

"He doesn't even count," Merry asserted. "That means you get one more."

Dolly had never thought of it that way before. Because she and Rooster had married in the church, it had always counted to her. But had it really? It certainly hadn't been any kind of real marriage.

"Think about what they're saying," Layla kindly advised. "You know I'm all for love at this stage of our lives."

"Here, here!" Merry picked up her glass and lifted it in a toast to later-in-life love.

Everyone set down their plates, cake annihilated, and toasted.

"Oh, oh," Ginger groaned. "There's Balls. I hoped we'd lost him."

"I wondered where he disappeared to," Merry said. "I haven't seen him since the ceremony."

Balls stood inside looking lost. He scanned the room, grabbed a plate of cake, noticed the girls, and came out to the balcony.

"Man, this place is the bomb, isn't it?" he said as he hoovered his cake, not bothering with a civilized fork, opting to eat with his fingers, instead.

"Balls," Dolly said as she studied him from head to toe, "did you take a shower in one of the guest rooms?"

"Sure." He swallowed hard to finish off his cake, licking his fingers after the last bite. "Why not? They've got so many bath-rooms, they'll never know. I needed a shower, bad."

"Believe me, we know," Ginger informed him.

"You do smell better," Merry offered.

"Thanks. The soap was kinda girly, but I like it."

"And that shirt," Dolly added. "It's clean and too big. Did you actually steal one of the groom's shirts out of his bedroom?"

"Sure. Why not? I mean, he's got a hundred of them in there."

"Excuse me."

They turned around to see an Elvis they hadn't seen before. This one was good. Very, very good. Dapper. An older Elvis, their age, but in the younger Elvis's more casual clothes, jeans and a leather jacket. This one was in great shape, which the real Elvis had not been at the time of his demise. This one also had fabulous white hair, which the real Elvis never would have allowed of himself, having become too fond of harsh black hair dye. This Elvis had mastered the original's signature crooked grin, which extracted a smile from all of them.

"I'm so happy to see you here," he said, the vibrato baritone voice pitch perfect. "You're the Burly-Q Girls who performed at the Flamingo tonight. I snuck in to watch the show from backstage and you were a wonderful surprise. You were fantastic. I had such a great time. Thank you. He broke into song, rolling one leg in and out and curling his upper lip like Elvis always did when he sang. "I want you, I need you, I love you …"

They clapped enthusiastically when he finished.

"Oh, that's wonderful!"

"Thank you!"

"You're great!"

"Did you perform yet at the conference?"

"No, I won't be performing. You see, I'm not an impersonator. I'm here tonight as a friend of Junior's."

Every eye roamed from him to Junior, who stood in the living room fawning over Annie, and back to him. They couldn't make the connection.

"Well, goodbye, Burly-Q Girls. It's been a pleasure." He bussed each of the women on the cheek, shook Balls' hand, and left.

"Wowzer. He's good. Best impersonator I've ever seen," Balls said.

"Yeah," Merry added, "he really sticks to his story, doesn't he?"

"Who sticks to his story?" Annie had walked over and asked the question.

"That Elvis impersonator." Ginger pointed to the elevator where the man had disappeared.

"Oh," Annie said, "That's no impersonator. That's the real Elvis."

"But he's dead," Dolly claimed.

"Oh, heavens, no he isn't. That's just a story he made up to get out of all the craziness in his life. He lives right here in Vegas. He and Pookie Junior have been friends forever, 'cuz Pookie has so much money."

"Nah. That can't be true." Ginger looked confused. "Could it?"

"Of course not." Dolly said it but wasn't sure she believed it.

"It's true," Annie insisted.

"Huh," was all Merry could manage.

"Stranger things have happened," Layla tossed out.

"Well," Betty quipped, "butter my biscuit. I just met Elvis Presley." She touched her cheek where he'd kissed her.

Balls snagged half a piece of cake Layla hadn't eaten off her plate and stuffed it into his mouth. "I don't know about that, but there's one thing for sure. Youse all is the real deal. No question about that. And we're a real family. And like a real family, I know you ain't crazy about every member." He pointed at himself. "But we're family anyway, like it or not. We grew up together in the business and we took care of each other. And here we are years later, takin' care of each other again. We'll find your money. We'll fix this mess. And we'll be one happy family again."

He slung an arm around Ginger's shoulder. She sloughed him off. He shrugged.

The Burly-Q Girls couldn't help but break into laughter. This might not be the ending they'd hope for, but it was an ending that promised a new beginning.

CHAPTER 21

*D*olly stretched her body in time to the soft, sexy saxophone that played jazz in the background. "O-o-oh, that was nice," she mewled.

"I agree." James' smoky voice belied his after-sex contentment.

They lay in his bed, naked, facing one another. A magnificent view of Lake Huron was visible outside the large window at the other end of his bedroom, but neither of them paid any attention to that. They only had eyes for one another.

"I think we did well for two people whose body parts don't all bend the way they used to," Dolly teased as she ran her palm down his chest.

"True. But the body parts that matter still do okay." He kissed the Burly-Q Girl tattoo on her upper arm.

"Yes, they do. Remember when you were young and were a virtual acrobat in the rack? I didn't know you then, but I'd bet anything you were."

"I do believe I was." He grinned. Ah, those lines down his cheeks got to her again and she traced one with her finger. "No doubt you were, too," he added.

"Uh huh. I confess, that was great fun. But the reason I brought I up is I wouldn't trade any of that for this. This is the best."

"Dolly, let's get married."

She paused. His statement didn't surprise her. In fact, she'd been expecting it considering they'd spent every possible moment together for the last month since she got home from Las Vegas. She'd been thinking about it and had decided she wanted to be happy again, with number three. With James. Giddy as a teenaged girl, she broke into a smile.

"Yes, James, I'll marry you."

She took him into her arms, and they gave it another go.

THE END ... for now.

AUTHOR'S NOTE

I hope this story inspired to do a little hoochie coochie dance yourself. Here's the link to my YouTube playlist that inspired me as I wrote: https://www.youtube.com/watch?v=m1FfpGwVqU8&list=PLQKe00q3CIyZ_2y8XQy-XN-6rofXkXJlu&index=21

If you'd like to leave a review for this novel, I am ever so grateful. Here's a direct link: https://Amazon.com/review/create-review?&asin=B09NRCXVMD

Link to review this book.

The next story in this trilogy is *The Burly-Q Girls: 6 Dicks,* where the troupe continues their amateur sleuthing. And Annie! Oh my, Annie manages to get into all kinds of good trouble. Here's that link: The Burly-Q Girls: 6 Dicks

ABOUT THE AUTHOR

Linda Hughes is a bestselling co-author and award-winning author of 20 books. When she was in college, she worked as a waitress in a house of burlesque. There she met Lottie the Body, the inspiration for this trilogy of stories.

You'll find her at: www.lindahughes.com